The Cat House

The Cat House

Anna J.
Brittani Williams
Laurinda D. Brown

Q-Boro Books
WWW.QBOROBOOKS.COM

An Urban Entertainment Company

Published by Q-Boro Books

ISBN-13: 978-1-933967-46-2
ISBN-10: 1-933967-46-3
LCCN: 2007933673

First Printing June 2008
Printed in the United States of America

10 9 8 7 6 5 4 3 2 1

Cover layout/design by Candace K. Cottrell; Photo by Torrance Williams
Editors: Candace K. Cottrell, Brian Sandy

Q-BORO BOOKS
Jamaica, Queens NY 11434
WWW.QBOROBOOKS.COM

Have you met the ladies of
The Cat House?

Visit **QBoroBooks.com/cathouse.htm** for character profiles, polls, and online exclusives!

A Message to Readers

Dear Readers,

The Cat House is a special experience. While reading this succulent story, I'm confident you will find the voices of all three authors to be different and exciting. This project was meant to take those distinct voices and allow them to complement each other through the continuation of a dramatic, erotic, and enticing read.

I hope that each and every one of you will embrace these differences while savoring the tale these talented authors have penned.

Enjoy!

Candace K. Cottrell, Editor

PART ONE

Lady Dee

BY ANNA J.

The Operation

"Dee, how are we going to break this down to Mr. Dixon? He doesn't seem excited about mixing up the two. And what about the girls? Wouldn't that cut into their pay?" Brandy asked me in a concerned voice, but I wasn't really worried about it. I knew how to make money, and it was definitely going to pop off once the changes I wanted were made.

"Earl is about getting his paper first, if nothing else. We just have to present it to him in the right way. I think the only girl we'll have a problem with is that damn Kimona, but she ain't but two steps from hitting the streets anyway so we'll deal with it then."

I'd been sitting there crunching numbers for the past three hours, and the slips still weren't adding up. Now, I'd like to think I was running a tight ship at Allure, and I pretty much had the girls in check.

Allure was a very exclusive gentleman's club where only the cream of the crop was invited to join. The clients were handpicked personally by Earl Dixon, a prominent

DC businessman who had a little bit of a kinky side himself. Usually he met his clients at corporate conferences where he booked future business for his Fortune 500 companies, one of which was located not too far from where we operated, near the White House.

Earl Dixon, at the age of fifty, definitely had his house in order. The seven-story building that housed Allure was made up of a mixture of all types of consumer traffic. On the first floor of the building you would find everything, from a dentist's office to a women's clinic where the Allure girls went for any checkups that were required. There were boutiques along the same corridor, and a small food court meant that the people who worked and lived in the building didn't have to go far for a meal.

On the second floor were more private offices for law firms, government businesses, and things of that nature where the traffic coming in and out was at a minimum. Most of the men who worked in those offices were clients of Allure, but everything was kept under wraps.

Membership to Allure could be extremely expensive, depending on the amount of attention you were paying for. The third floor was made up of one- and two-bedroom apartments that Earl Dixon rented out to regular people looking for a place to stay and to clients of the club who needed a hideaway from their wives when they wanted to creep out.

The fourth and fifths floor housed the club and sex rooms where the men were taken for special treatment. The elevator that let you up to the floor worked by a special key card that was delivered to you by one of the girls on the day you were to come to the house. Earl worked out a deal with FedEx to provide a few uniforms for the girls so that no one would be suspicious of the packages that were being dropped off. The key card is sent in a FedEx envelope so that only the owner would know what it is, and the girls were rotated every so often so that the same one didn't keep showing up at our clients' jobs.

The key card allowed them access upstairs, so once the doors opened the key was turned in to myself, Lady Dee, or Brandy, my assistant. Those clients that only came for the atmosphere and conversation were given a gold bracelet with a black medallion hanging from it. This let us know immediately what part of the house they were allowed into, because if you are only there to talk, what reason did you have to be upstairs in the sex rooms? We had private areas where the girls took those clients who needed a shoulder to cry on, and once the key was turned back in, they could go and get drinks and do whatever they were there for.

Clients that came for sex were given one of two bracelets. For rooms with basic services from the girls these guys received a white gold bracelet with our trademark black medallion hanging from it. They were granted entrance to the part of the house beyond the bar and lounge area, where they could fall back for a little while with their working girl before going up to one of the sex rooms designated for that level of service.

If the client was wearing a platinum bracelet, he would be housed in a luxury suite, where a relaxing massage by as many girls as he wanted to join in was given. And if he had a particular fetish, we had themed rooms set up for that as well. The platinum member pretty much had free reign as to what he wanted to go down, where it was somewhat limited to other members. Once you signed up, you had to stay at that level for six months before you could move up to a higher ranking in the house.

Everything was prepaid before the client got there, so the only thing they would need cash for was to tip the girls and to pay for extra time, drinks, and/or any stimulants required to perform. So that there wasn't a paper trail, we issued a prepaid credit card to the guys that can only be reloaded with a credit card on a monthly basis to keep the club discreet. It showed up as clothing purchase on the credit card receipt to keep everything top secret, and the balance had to be paid in full for the service when the date was set. No one could just stop by, because you never knew who you would see inside of Allure. That's why we went by appointment only.

Last, but certainly not least, you had to know the code. The word *allure* means to attract or tempt by something flattering or desirable. When coming into Allure, everything about it was definitely desirable, and you had to know what you wanted. Upon entry the client was asked three simple questions: What's your desire? What are your inhibitions? What do want to change upon leaving here? If it worked with us, we worked with you, and at the end of the day, everyone was happy.

The women who worked there were the cream of the crop, and all were checked for disease by the gynecologist in the building. Some were aspiring models and some former pole-dancers, but they were flawless in every aspect. As a rule, none of the women had kids, nor were they attached to anyone, to keep complicated situations at a minimum. I didn't have time to deal with jealous husbands and boyfriends because just like at any nine-to-five, we had money to make, and time is money. They also had to be drug-free, although they were allowed to serve the clients ecstasy pills or whatever they needed to relax, but they were not allowed to partake themselves, so they were always able to be in control of their situation.

Five top girls worked amongst the twenty-five girls resided within Allure. Sasha was a dark chocolate beauty who stood about five-six with an extremely curvy body. She had the kind of ass you can see from the front, and the clients were loving every inch of her slightly voluptuous frame. She was one of the few girls that could ride a pole from the top, and anything went with her, so it was easier to market her to potential new clients. It didn't matter whether it was a man or woman, anal or vaginal, group sex or solo, she was down for whatever and would go to extreme measures to please her clients. So she was definitely a top pick.

Another one of my girls was Holly. I kept her around for those that liked white chocolate. This chick could take anything you threw at her, including the S&M clients that she loved to beat on. Candle wax and dildos were her favorites, and she had a certain DC senator turned out for months off this move she called "the lemon twist. "

Amber and Desire were making good money also, but the one working girl that was knocking them all out the box was Kimona. She looked like she could be Dominican and black with long, jet-black hair that fell well past her shoulders. Her bronzed skin looked kissed by the sun, and everyone who came in loved her slanted eyes. I rarely had to put her in a lineup because she was always busy with a client when I called for everyone to be present.

Kimona walked around like she knew she was the shit, too. That's why I stayed in her ass the way I did. I mean, she was definitely making money, and I'll even go as far as saying she brought in the most money in the house.

But we didn't pay the bills solely on her income, and lately she'd been smelling herself. She was showing up late for appointments. That confused the hell out of me because she lived right there in the building, which was a courtesy that was extended by Dixon so the girls would always have a safe place to stay. That's not to say that they couldn't have a life outside of the walls, because what they did on their time was on them, but when it came to make it pop, they had better be there to pop it.

In order to become a resident in Allure's apartments, you had to get a ranking of four out of five from your clients for the first thirty days after you were hired, and even after you got in you had to maintain the quota that was set for you on a monthly basis to secure your spot or it would be given to someone else. It was sort of like a probation period where we tested them to see if they had what we wanted. There were twenty-five girls working at any given time, and even though there was room to house all of them, we didn't. Newbies had to especially work hard to stay, and I noticed Kimona started wilding out when Torri, the newest working girl, came on board. It wasn't not unlike Kimona to get uptight when someone new came through, but when this girl showed up, her entire attitude did a total one-eighty. I had to warn her on several occasions that her funky-ass attitude was going to find her on the street, and I could see that I'd have to show her better than I could tell her.

As a rule, all men who were entertained were handled within the walls of Allure, but from what Torri told me, little Miss Kimona had been seeing men in her apartment, a blatant violation of the rules we had set for the girls that resided there. It was almost like stealing company time at a nine-to-five, and the repercussions of that were immediate termination.

Now, I wasn't the type of madam to take someone's word for straight value, but when things were brought to my attention, I would start to investigate. After all, Torri was a new girl trying to land a permanent home at Allure, and it seemed as if she would do whatever to get in. Kimona knew the rules though, so I would really be disappointed if what Torri said was true, but I needed to have my facts straight first before stepping to her.

Another problem I was having with her was that her slips weren't adding up. All slips were turned in at the end of the night from the bars and the "lab" where pills were distributed, and all of the prices for service were basic, unless you wanted something extra. At that moment you would pay your working girl for the services, drinks, pills, etc. Her job was to then take whatever monies she'd collected to Brandy to be put into her total made for the month. From what I'd been hearing, Kimona had been collecting money for extra services and ordering drinks and e-pills for her clients, but the money wasn't reflecting that on her receipt. That was the equivalent of stealing company time, and now you're taking money out of the petty cash box.

Kimona was wilding out, but I had something for her ass. The girls that were employed by Earl Dixon were paid well, and they had no reason to be sneaky or to be stealing. I didn't want to go to Earl until I had solid facts, because ultimately it was his decision to remove a girl from the house. He'd found Kimona in a strip club, and that's exactly where her ass would be once I found out what was really going on. Earl left me to run shit while he handled his business. If Kimona kept testing me, she'd soon find out why I was called The Enforcer, and I would have bet my life that she wasn't going to like the outcome.

The Induction

"Brandy, tell Torri to meet us in the chambers. It's about time she get broken in . . ."

Torri, the newest to Allure, had been there for about two weeks, and it was time she saw what it was really hitting for. Kimona was on her way out the door, and I knew Torri was waiting to jump into her spot, but I had to see if she had what it takes to really do what we needed her to do around here. I also wanted to know how she felt about the opposite sex being of service here as well. Most of the girls weren't feeling it, and I was still trying to decide if it was worth the hassle. Who felt like being in a house full of angry bitches?

The chamber was a room that we used for those clients that liked S&M treatments. I chose my top four girls (Sasha, Holly, Amber, and Desire) to participate in the induction. I needed to see exactly what Torri would allow, and how far she was really willing to go.

The room was set up sort of like a dungeon in a castle.

There was a wall that your submissive could be chained to that turned into a table when laid flat, and we offered costumes to the girls that the clients paid for if they were requesting a fantasy. Whips, chains, and cock rings were the set themes for these types of parties. I knew this would be the perfect spot to test Torri's limits and to also allow the girls to have some fun with her.

When she came into the room she had that dear-trapped-in-headlights look that made me almost burst into laughter, but I knew I had to keep a straight face. Here at Allure we didn't have too many rules, but the number one rule was simple: You had to be freaky. If you were coming in with all kinds of inhibitions like being scared to suck a dick, then you would be one of the brokest bitches around, and I had no use for you. We had a few that were scared of the girl-on-girl thing, but once again, that defeated the purpose. It was about what the client wanted, and we were there to please.

My girls already knew what to do, wasting no time strapping her to the wall by her ankles and wrists. I took a seat in the corner with my camcorder in hand, the record button already pressed. I made it a point to tape the inductions so if I couldn't be there for the entire thing I could see it later. I didn't need any accidental deaths and shit like that from the girls taking things too far. I also did it as a safety precaution in case one of the girls wanted to play the victim and try to press charges or something. Nothing was forced upon them, and my proof was that tape.

"So, Torri, how do you like working here at Allure?" I asked as I circled around her now naked and bound body.

Torri had a firm ass that bounced when she walked.

Her breasts had dark, kissable nipples, and her stomach was completely flat. She wore her hair in a wrap that pointed into a *V* in the center of her back. Taking a paddle from the table on my way around, I held it high in the air and swung my arm in a swift motion, connecting with the tender flesh that formed her round ass. She flinched a little, but kept her stance straight. Come to find out, she was a little tougher than I thought.

"I love it here at Allure, where we have charm and sex appeal," she said, spouting the company motto like she'd been saying it all her life.

As I continued to walk a circle around her, the girls began a slow torture of her body. It was all-out from there, and we would see if she were truly made for this place.

By the time I had gotten around to the front with a chain hanging from the middle of her body, Sasha had fastened nipple-pinchers to Torri's breasts. She had her eyes closed, I guess, to try and cope with the pain, but when you're in a room with a client, it's about their fantasy, and they don't care if it hurts or not.

I stood in front of her, watching her facial expressions while Holly and Amber worked dildos from the anal/vaginal position on the floor. Torri's face was a mixture of pleasure and pain, and I was curious as to when she was going to break. I took the chain in my hand and pulled it lightly, producing a low moan from her. The skin around her nipples was bright red and felt warm under my fingertips when I lightly squeezed her breasts for reaction. She was doing good, surprisingly, so it was time to step the game up a notch.

Pushing her body back to the connecting leather mattress, I connected the two so that Torri's body could lay flat down. Relieving her of the nipple-pinchers, I went to light several candles around the room while Desire and Sasha soothed her bruised nipples with their tongues.

When Torri came here she'd said she was a cum-squirter, so I needed to see if that statement was true as well. Men liked nasty shit that was out of the ordinary, and that would definitely be a way for her to climb the ladder quickly at Allure. My top girls weren't top because they had good pussy; you had to know a trick or three to make top rankings.

I kept candle wax on warmers so that we could always have it ready when it was time to play. Taking out enough clear plastic flutes for all of us, I filled them with different colors of wax. Handing all the girls a cup, we stood in a circle around Torri's naked body. Sasha had a vibrator buzzing against her clit, and I found it hilarious that she tried to close her legs and she was bound.

Starting in the space between her breasts, I began to drizzle the hot wax down Torri's body, producing more moans from her. All of the women followed behind me, pouring their wax on her as well. As I stood back I could see wax dripping from the silver hoop that pierced her clit, and it shook as her body moved around on the table.

"How do you feel about men working here, Torri?" I asked her as I poured my refilled cup over her body. Her face showed that she was close to orgasm, and I wanted to see what this squirting business was all about.

"The more the merrier."

"The more the merrier, she says." I laughed out loud as I talked to the girls. That was good to know because there were changes that needed to be made, and I needed to see who I would be keeping around and who I would be kicking the hell out.

Picking up an electric vibrator from the table, I held it

up to the wax-covered ring. Her entire body tensed up and her eyes rolled into the back of her head,

"Uh-oh, ladies . . . I think she's about to blow," I said, smiling as I pressed the vibrator harder onto her clit, causing a stream of cum to shoot from her and land on the floor a few feet away. Satisfied that she could perform, I gave the girls the OK to loosen her bonds and have some fun with her before leaving the room.

As fun as that was, I still had issues with Kimona to deal with. I had to send her down to the medical office to get tested for drugs, because what other reason would she have to steal? We only offered pills in the lab at Allure, and they were off-limits to the girls, so she had to be tripping off of cocaine or something. This was truly out of character for her, and I just couldn't wrap my head around the fact that she was acting a fool. I mean, she made over a hundred thousand dollars last year. Tax free, I might add. The only money being taken from her pay was to cover doctor's expenses. She didn't have to pay for room and board because Earl took care of everything, and we paid taxes like we were running a legitimate business, so everything was cool. I came to the conclusion that the bitch was just being greedy.

It was kind of quiet in the house today. The tapping of my heels on the marble floor echoed as I walked through the hall. A quick glance at my watch showed that I had a new client due to show up in about five minutes. The first thing I did was check my books in the office to see who was available before looking at the client's chart to see what he wanted. He joined as a platinum member, so that showed me that he wasn't afraid to spend his money. I usually gave those members to Kimona because she always showed them a good time, but it was time I taught her a lesson, and I knew she was available for lineup today, so this was going to be good.

Pressing the button on the underside of my desk, I summoned the girls to the foyer to line up for our new guests. I personally liked for them to be ready for the client when they got off the elevator so that he could see what we had to offer from the very beginning.

Within seconds the women began to fall in line, and Kimona was among them, a smug look on her face. Just before the guy came up, I informed the girls that he was a new platinum member and normally I would just push him toward Kimona, but today it wasn't going down like that. My expression matched hers, as our new guest arrived, and I had to smile at my lineup. I had some of the best girls in DC, and Earl made sure of that. The only girls who weren't in the lineup were those who had scheduled appointments within the next two hours.

A handsome Puerto Rican exited the elevator dressed in a crisp Brooks Brothers suit, and Ferragamo loafers that looked brand spanking new. The baby blue button-down shirt he wore under his blazer was opened to reveal a smooth washboard stomach. The platinum Allure bracelet on his wrist was nice and shiny against his black suit, and I could see the women salivating, hoping to get picked.

"Welcome. We aim to fulfill your every fantasy. Here at Allure we have charm and sex appeal," the women spoke in unison, bringing a smile to the guest's face.

"Here at Allure,"—I walked out from behind the podium to stand next to him—"we have charm and sex appeal. Who do you request this evening?" I asked him in a sultry voice, taking his guest pass from his hand.

He looked like he couldn't decide, and normally at this

point I'd be pointing him to Kimona, but a lesson had to be learned.

The client walked up and down the corridor, looking at the women carefully. Kimona had a look on her face that said she knew she would be chosen. I simply stood to the side, hoping he would skip past her thieving ass. After walking back and forth six or seven times he chose three girls from the lineup, leaving Kimona standing there looking stupid. The smirk I had on my face mocked the scorn she had on hers, and once the client walked off, she stalked off to the elevator, rolling her eyes at me as the door closed. Ask me if I gave a damn. Steal from me, and I'll cut all of your funds dead short. Short funds meant that she wouldn't meet the quota, and not meeting the quota meant she had to go. Fuck with me, and you'll get fucked. Believe that.

Shortly after, three more platinum clients arrived for their appointments. They selected the rest of the girls, and when one of the guys asked for Kimona, I told him she wasn't available and pointed him toward Torri.

My logic was if Kimona wanted to make money, she wouldn't have stormed off. You had to maintain a certain quota to stay in the house, and since she was taking sides and skimming money, she'd be out the door in no time. Smiling slyly, I went to my office to prepare for a more private appointment. I was interviewing possible male workers to come into the house. I wanted to at least have a lineup for Earl when I presented him with the layout I had to expand business. Earl wanted to see figures, and I was sure, once I showed him the benefits, we would be able to move forward.

"Brandy." I buzzed into the intercom connected to the front desk, where she was updating the database to match sales from the receipts.

"Go 'head," she came back, knowing I was about to request something of her.

"Have someone bring me a shot of Hpnotiq. That damn girl got my nerves frazzled."

She didn't even respond, but I knew it was on the way. I was looking forward to the interviews because I knew they would get physical. After all, I had to make sure they could perform, right? There were plenty of female clients who were willing to pay for sex, and once I got Earl to see things my way, we'd really be rolling in the dough.

The Prospects

Within hours I was sitting across from Hot Chocolate, a male dancer from the Boy Wonder all-male review I met in Atlantic City a while back. Brandy and I were asked to accompany Earl down there on a hunt for new pussy.

As a rule, no client stays overnight. They are allowed to come and enjoy the woman, but they have to leave after their two hours are up, or pay for more time. Although everyone in the house was constantly tested for all STDs and communicable diseases, the clients had to wear a condom. That part is non-negotiable. One of these simple bitches got so high that she allowed a client to have unprotected sex with her, and she got pregnant. I got rid of her. We tried to maintain a certain number of girls at all times, so we were out looking for the next best thing.

While in the club I ended up chatting with another woman, who told me she was heading over to a male strip show. Earl was enjoying the advantages of the VIP rooms, so after sending him a note that Brandy and I would meet him back at the hotel, we followed the woman over to The 40/40 Club, where the all-male review was being held.

When we walked in, the place was packed to capacity with horny women waiting for the show to begin. I saw several of the women counting out their money, just waiting for the first of the ten men who would be performing for their touching, tasting, and viewing pleasure. Just seeing these women so eager to put their money up for strange men made me wonder how much Allure could benefit from that kind of money in a more controlled situation. I was sure, given the right circumstances, a woman would pay for sex, but how did I get it to be appealing?

The M.C., a plus-sized chick with a commanding voice, had the room up on their feet, hyped up about the coming attractions we were supposed to be fortunate to see. Hot Chocolate was the first to come out, and just the looks of him had me ready to peel from the stack of hundreds I had in my right pocket. He was the color of hot chocolate with a shot of milk in it, and the length of his dick made my mouth fall dead open. I thought for sure they were stuffing their thongs with something, but he came completely out of his, and all of his sweet chocolate goodness stood at attention. It swung back and forth between his legs as he gyrated around the stage, seemingly hypnotizing the audience.

I was amazed at the strength of his body and the agility with which he moved. You could tell that he had been doing this forever, but something was missing from his eyes. We were seated right next to the stage, and I could see everything. His face showed that he was happy to be there, but his eyes . . . they looked like his mind was in another state. He did a striptease that left me speechless, and soon every woman was waving her hard-earned money in the air for a three-second lap dance that would only last long enough for her to get home and pretend her man was like the man that was on stage. I needed this kind of money coming into Allure. I just had to get my mind together so I could execute the plan.

When he got around to Brandy and me, she was all heated and dropping money like she had it like that. He pushed up on me, and the feel of his hardness against my thigh almost made me break, but this was about business. Instead of putting money in his G-string I slid him my business card, letting him know before he danced off to the next horny female that we should work together.

Sitting across from me now, gone was that lost-in-space look I saw onstage. Before me sat confidence and sex appeal packaged in an Armani suite. His teeth looked like he lived at the orthodontist, and he had just enough Angel cologne to arouse my senses but not be overpowering.

"So, what do you think you can add to the walls of Allure? Why would a woman want to pay you for sex?" I threw the questions at him back-to-back to see how he could handle himself. I'd been questioning him since he'd walked in the door, and so far he was doing his thing.

Instead of answering, he stood up from his seat and locked my office door. I didn't say a word, my face set like stone, my curiosity played around my eyes on the low. He never broke eye contact, and his body moved in a rhythm that only he could hear as he took his sweet time removing his clothes and neatly folding them in the chair he'd been sitting in.

I acted like I didn't see the gold Magnum condom wrapper he slyly slipped from his pants pocket before placing them over the chair on top of his jacket, but my pussy was drenching my seat, and I involuntarily began to squirm. *It's about to be on,* I thought. And it had been a while, so I hoped he wasn't just a sexy package with no stroke game.

Circling my desk, he pulled me from the chair and carried me in his arms, setting me down on the edge of my desk. The short skirt I wore rose up around my waist, and the heat radiated from between my legs. I could feel his dick pressing up against the material of my thong, but I was a pro, so I acted like it didn't faze me in the least. He did a slow grind against my clit that almost made me moan. Almost. But the thing is, he needed to know that a grind wasn't enough. It didn't really mean a thing if all he had left were two strokes and a shudder once he put his dick in.

I gave him my most bored stare, hopefully letting him know that I wasn't fazed. He pushed my thong to the side, and the side of his index finger rubbed against the wetness on my clit, causing a chill to course through my body. He smiled and continued to finger my swollen clit, but that wouldn't be enough to make me cum.

With his free hand he secured the condom over his length and used the head of his dick to tease my opening. He had me at that point, because I had been wanting to feel him inside me since the day I laid eyes on him.

There were rules, though, and I didn't want him to feel like he would have access to me like that. More than likely this would be the last time he even got within sniffing distance of my pussy because we had money to make. That is, once I sold Earl on it, and it would be a lot easier to pitch an idea that I'd already sampled than one on a maybe. The girls I hired went through the same ritual. If you couldn't please me, you couldn't please anyone.

Just the head of his dick was stretching my opening to

the limit, but I needed to feel all of him. I wanted to know if he could reach the back. I still wore a bored expression on my face, but I was dripping steadily down the side of my desk. He pulled out, but on the comeback he gave it all to me, causing me to loose my breath. He was hitting me with hard, deep strokes that caught me way off guard, and all I could do was hold on to the edges of the desk for dear life, pissed for a quick second because all of my papers were now on the floor and it would take me forever to put them in order again.

"You thought this was a game, huh? You didn't think big daddy would wear that ass out?" he asked into my shoulder, pressing his body down on mine, making me lie flat down on the desk. He pushed my legs back to my ears and climbed up on the desk, drilling into me non-stop.

"Damn, this pussy is tight. You want big daddy to cum?" he asked while getting up on his knees and pulling my body up toward him, throwing my legs up on his shoulders.

I screamed for him not to cum, in between sucking on my own nipples, and he drilled into me. The feel of his balls slapping against my ass made me feel like I was about to cum.

He looked like he was getting mad because I wouldn't answer. Hopping off the desk, he dragged me to the edge again and rolled me over so that my ass was up in the air and I was standing on the tips of my toes to keep my balance. He spread my legs wider than I was accustomed to, got up under me in a squatting position like I was riding him backwards, and pushed up into me with all his might. I was bouncing my ass on him like it was a basketball, and he was meeting me stroke for stroke.

I was getting into it something fierce until I felt his finger invade my asshole. I flinched for a second, but I was cool. This is the kind of shit that would have a client turned out, so I let him do his thing.

With his free hand he squeezed my breasts and pinched my nipples, dicking me down with a constant rhythm.

"Mmm . . . I'm about to cum," I said to him as my body began to tense up. He was tearing my G-spot to pieces, and I couldn't take it anymore.

"Oh yeah, you about to cum, huh? Now you can talk?"

I couldn't respond because my orgasm was so close, and in a few more strokes it would be on. I arched my back and bounced my ass harder on his dick, squeezing my pussy muscles so tight, it felt like I was hurting him. My breath became shorter, and I started moving faster.

I was almost home when this nigga pulled out. I turned around just in time for him to jerk his dick a few times and cum all over my damn shirt. To say I was pissed would me putting it mildly. I couldn't believe he pulled out and I was so close to cumming.

"Why did you stop?" I asked in a high-pitched voice because I couldn't quite get my bearings, and my pussy was still pulsating. My walls were clinching, and my body wouldn't stop shaking.

"Oh, so now you can talk, huh?" Hot Chocolate said, quickly taking over the situation. He pushed me up on the edge of the desk and stood between my legs. He lightly pinched my clit. I closed my eyes instantly, my orgasm threatening to rush through.

"What you want big daddy to do, huh? You wanna cum?"

"Yes," I said through clenched teeth. It was right there; all he had to do was finger my pussy and it would be over.

He must have read my mind because he stuck his first two fingers into me and used his thumb to rub my clit.

Within minutes I was screaming and moaning at the top of my lungs, soaking his hand completely. He had a smug look on his face that I wanted to slap off, but I couldn't even be mad. He definitely had swagger.

"So, do I got the job?" he asked while getting dressed and going right back to his professional mannerisms.

I looked at him for a second and knew that I had to get him up in here. He would make a killing.

"What if a man came in and requested your services? What would you do?" I asked him as I wiped my shirt off. I threw that out there just to see if he would take the bait.

"I'm not gay," he said with a straight face.

"But would you do him?"

"If he paid for it."

"I'll get back to you in a couple of weeks. See Brandy on your way out to make sure she has your info."

I didn't even make eye contact, instead gathering my papers from the floor. My body was still tingling. A woman wouldn't even need two hours with him, but there were still some things I had to be sure of. If he didn't eat pussy he was as useless as a girl who didn't suck dick. Yeah, I would definitely need to see about getting him up in here. It was just a matter of time.

Meanwhile, I still had three other guys to interview. A small smile spread across my lips when I thought about all the money I would be pulling in. Once I talked to Earl, everything would be good.

The Pitch

"So you see, Earl, it would be very beneficial to Allure. Women have a freaky side, and every so often we need some side action as well." I'd been trying to get Earl to see me on this male performer issue, but he wasn't having it. When his mind was made up, it was hard trying to change it.

"Women just get so emotional. They don't know how to separate the two. Dee, you're a woman, so you already know these things. Besides that, we can't operate on an every-so-often situation. Bills don't get paid every so often, so we don't have room for those kinds of choices."

Earl came to look at the books, and I had all of Kimona's stuff set to the side to show him the problem I was having with her. I couldn't really go on what Torri saw, but I knew I would have to start popping up in her room during the night. What I did have proof of was the receipts not adding up. The slips from the bars and lab didn't add up to what her turned-in slips amounted to, and I had her sitting in my office waiting for Earl and I to come in. He wanted to look at all the rooms, and I had to line the girls up so he could see that everything was in working order. His favorite girl was acting a fool, and he didn't seem to happy about that.

"Not all women are like that, Earl. I think a woman can handle the situation. It's the guy that gets emotional. Maybe we could do a test run. I'll help you pick the women."

"Let me think about it some more," Earl said to me in a dismissive fashion, as if he was done with the situation altogether. "Now let's handle this Kimona situation. I am not pleased with what I've been hearing."

I briefly ran down what I'd been hearing from the other girls and that problem I had with her slips coming up short. He looked almost hurt, but kept his face straight. She was, after all, our top working girl, and I couldn't believe that she had stooped to this level. I finished up my report of Kimona's wrongdoing just as we approached my office door. I gave him a grim look before I opened it, hoping that he would just kick her out of the house.

When we walked in Kimona had her feet propped up on my desk and her chair reclined back with her eyes closed. She jumped up when she noticed Earl in the door because I'd just told her I wanted to talk to her. I never told her I was bringing Earl with me. I'm sure she had all kinds of smart shit to say, but with Earl present she would keep it professional.

Closing the door behind him, he took a seat behind my desk, and I took the seat next to Kimona, readying myself for war. I felt a little embarrassed because of the activities that took place on my desk, and I didn't want Earl to touch anything.

He looked through the paperwork I had on Kimona and the frown in his brow was not a good thing. "So, Kimona, what do you have to say for yourself?" Earl asked, making eye contact with Kimona before looking at me.

I kept my mouth shut and decided it was best to let her dig a hole for herself.

"What is there to say? I'm being framed for something I didn't do. I think Lady Dee just wants me out of the house because she's jealous," she answered, with way more attitude than Earl and I were expecting.

"Jealous? Of you? Little girl, you must have me twisted with someone that actually gives a damn about you. It's not that serious for me, trust and believe." I threw the attitude right back. This chick didn't want it with me. I would make her feel like I was her worst nightmare come true, and she'd want to leave on her own.

"Ladies, let's try to handle this in a civilized manner." Earl tried to diffuse the situation, but I was cool. I was the one who controlled the workflow around here. Fuck with me and she'd be back at the strip club dancing for dollars.

"The slips show that you're not turning in all of your receipts," he said to Kimona, while sifting through the folder of her activities I had on the desk.

"The slips show that she's been getting work from the lab and drinks on her clients' tabs but hasn't been turning in receipts for those items. I talked to a couple of her clients, and they said that they never even requested lab services and felt uncomfortable about seeing her again. I've been sending them to Torri, the new girl who just started a few weeks ago."

Kimona's head whipped around so fast, she could have

snapped her neck in three places. She didn't know I was giving her clients to other people, and since she especially didn't like Torri, I knew it hit home. For the first time since Kimona had been employed at Allure, I saw her look a little nervous. Either shape up or ship out, because for a man pussy doesn't have a face, and just like they were paying her, they would pay the next chick that came by.

"Mr. Dixon, I know you are not going to let her do this to me. I'm the best girl you got! I bring the most money in here!" Kimona yelled at the top of her voice, and I smiled to myself on the inside because I finally had her bourgeois ass.

"Well, Kimona, the books don't lie," Earl said, glancing between us and the folder spread out in front of him.

I knew Earl wasn't nearly as upset as he pretended to be, but Kimona would definitely have to learn a lesson.

"Mr. Dixon, please. I know I messed up, but I'm good here. I can make you lots of money."

"This is what we'll do," he said looking at me in a nonchalant fashion.

I already knew what was coming next.

"Dee, she'll be on a thirty-day probation. That will give you, Kimona, enough time to make up the money that you weren't turning in. Plus, you have to meet your quota for the month. If both are not met, your belongings will be on the curb."

Kimona didn't even bother to respond, opting to leave the room instead.

I was thankful that Earl found time to stop by because I rarely ever saw him. He pretty much left the running of Allure to me, and since I had Brandy there to help me I rarely got a problem.

I allowed Earl to look through the folder once more before I brought up the male worker situation again. I figured if I kept beating him in the head with it, he'd at least let me show him a lineup.

"Let me see the men you're talking about and your marketing plan, and we'll take it from there, OK?"

"Yes, that's fine with me," I said to him, trying not to look overly elated. I only wanted to bring in three to five guys, and I would get potential clients who were professionals just like the men he brought in. Maybe even do some couples stuff to double the money.

After Earl left I called to set up appointments for two more potential men to work in the house. Hot Chocolate set the bar pretty high, so whoever came through had to really bring it. Supreme said he could be at the house by ten that night after he did a birthday party, and I hoped he'd take the time to shower before he got here. There's nothing worse than a sweaty-ass man trying to be all up in your face, and I didn't like a greasy man either.

Just as promised he arrived at ten on the nose, and I invited Brandy in for the interview to see what he was capable of. Oftentimes with the girls, a man would pick two of them. Strippers were used to crowds when all they had to do was grind on a few people and collect their cash while they were moving, but I wanted to see if he really had it in him to please two or more women at the same time.

He was definitely nice when we saw him up close. The name Supreme worked for him because his body definitely looked like a prime cut of beef. He wasn't overly muscular, but he was definitely on point. His eyes were a funny shade of gray that gave him a mischievous look that I was totally feeling, and Brandy didn't look like she was having a hard time adjusting at all.

He stood in between both of us and began unbuttoning our shirts, and I was proud that my breasts still stood at attention, although my stomach was not as flat as it used to be. Brandy had a gorgeous body as well.

After lifting our breasts from our bras, he took turns licking and sucking on our nipples until we were both panting and barely able to stand.

I don't remember seeing him moving the chairs back, but both of them were blocking the doorway, and I was sitting with my legs straddled across the arms of my chair with his face buried deep between my legs. Brandy was lying on the floor under him giving him a hand job and juggling his testicles in her mouth, a technique that she always used when we did a threesome, and one our loving boss Earl never got enough of.

His head game was the truth, and I came quickly. That was a good quality to have because women wanted to cum several times, and if you could get her to bust quick, that was a plus. But at the end of the day, good head wasn't enough. He had to have length, girth, and stamina to make it pop. A good rhythm never hurt either.

The pulling on my clit pushed my body to the edge of my seat every time I felt his lips make contact with my body. I was grinding my pussy into his face to match his rhythm and was getting closer and closer to my orgasm, and I wanted to stop him because I didn't want to cum like that, but my body wouldn't let me. Brandy was still working her magic, and I was trying to get control of the situation but it was getting difficult.

Finally pushing him back, I opened my eyes to see Brandy licking my juice off of his glazed face, and that shit turned me on. Laying her down on the floor, I slid from the chair and crawled up to her on all fours, resting my face between her legs. We'd done this a million times, and knew how to make each other cum. I pushed my ass up in the air and used my hands to spread my ass cheeks so that he could get in my pussy without complication. A pro would take the liberty of sticking his finger in my ass, so I'd just see what he would do. If he went there I'd know he was a keeper.

I could hear him rip open a condom wrapper, and that was another point for him because I didn't have to tell him to put one on. That meant that he would most likely practice safe sex with the clients, and that was our number-one rule. A glance to the side showed a gold Magnum wrapper, and since I didn't get a chance to see what he was working with I hoped the Magnum was a true fit.

I tensed up when the head of his dick touched me, and I let go of my ass cheek with my right hand so that I could spread my pussy lips for him and stroke my clit. Don't sleep on my skills, though, because I never lost rhythm with the job I was doing on Brandy, and she had her nipples in her mouth and her legs spread in a V.

When I stuck my tongue inside of her I could feel her walls pulsate, and I knew she was about to explode. I sucked on her clit like I was giving her a little mini blowjob, taking her clit into my mouth and sucking it up, letting it go before doing it again. She loved that shit, and I knew that would put her over the edge.

Meanwhile, Supreme had all that thick dick in me, stretching my walls to the max and trying to knock the bottom out my ass. Just as I suspected, he pushed his middle finger into my asshole, and was pinching on my nipples with his free hand.

This one wasn't a talker like Hot Chocolate, and that was cool because everyone didn't like that shit. He made me cum at the same time I was making Brandy cum, and I felt like I was riding on cloud nine. We switched positions so that he was laying flat on the floor. Brandy was squatting over his face, and he devoured her without hesitation. It was only fair that she got to feel the tongue like I did, and she would be getting some of his dick too, so we could make a mutual decision on whether we would be keeping him around or not. It was supposed to go down like that with Hot Chocolate too, but he snuck his ass up on me and I didn't have time to call her in.

Riding his dick was like sitting on a stiff pole, only, this one had a pulse. I bounced up and down on him, but I couldn't come all the way down because he was extra long. I came about three times before me and Brandy switched positions so that she could feel heaven like I was feeling it.

Taking her spot on his lips, I bent at the knees in a squatting position, using Brandy's breasts to keep balance. I brushed my thumbs across her nipples in a swift motion, causing them to harden and a moan to escape from her lips. She was good at riding and was tearing the dick up. I got up to give him time to breathe, because from the noises he was making it sounded like it was about to pop off.

Brandy stood up off his dick, clenching her muscles so that the condom slid off as she stood up. We both got on either side of him and gave him head at the same time while playing with his balls and jerking him off at the same time until he squirted a steady stream into the air, which landed on his stomach.

We looked down at him panting and moaning, trying to get his shit together, and a smile came over both of our faces. He was damn good at what he did, and I knew Brandy would agree that he should be on the team.

Stepping over him, we both got dressed so we could continue the interview. Besides, we had a few more guys coming in this week, and I wanted to get a lineup soon so we'd have something to present to Earl. We also had to decide how we would get clients in the doors, and I thought I had just the person to help bring them in.

"So, you'll be hearing from us soon, Supreme," I said to him while he gathered his belongings from the floor. Brandy had already left, and I played like I didn't care whether he stayed or went.

"Did you cum? Did you enjoy yourself?" Supreme asked once he was fully dressed and back in his seat.

The look I gave him could have killed him, and he looked uncomfortable all of a sudden. This was another part of the test to decide if he would get caught up in his emotions.

"If you have to ask, you already know the answer. You'll be hearing from me either way on a few days."

He looked unsure of himself for a second, but once he stood up he had his swagger back and that sealed the deal.

You had to be confident when dealing with clients, because if you left them with doubts it could be a potential loss. Although we were a discreetly operated company, clients sometimes brought friends for business, and we didn't need a bad rep.

After he left my thoughts turned to Kimona. I needed her ass out, and I knew just the thing that would get it done. I just had to make a phone call. Torri was more than ready to take her place, and it would just be a matter of time until it happened. On the day it did, I would gladly pack up Kimona's shit and set it on the damn curb.

The Setup

Since Kimona didn't deny stealing money from Allure, I knew I had to set her ass up good. I knew enough about her to know that she wouldn't willingly leave Allure because she was making way too much money, but under unusual circumstances she might just walk up out the joint. I had Brandy keep an eye on her to let me know when she was leaving, so I could go into her apartment.

Kimona had a nice spot, decorated by yours truly with touches of her own personal belongings. I had a client that came through for Holly. He was a detective in the bureau. I spoke with him over cocktails one night when I first heard that Kimona was sneaking clients into her room, and he was able to provide me with small cameras that could record up to a week's worth of footage to install around her apartment. I made sure he got the best treatment of his life that night. It ended up with him having to call a cab to go home because he was too drunk to drive. He liked anal penetration, so I know he probably woke up sore as hell the next day after messing around with Amber and Desire.

Waiting about ten minutes after Kimona left to make sure she wouldn't double back, I went into her place and planted the cameras in the living room so I could get a good view of whomever she had coming through. I needed to know if she was indeed inviting clients in or someone she had met on the street. Either way it was a violation of the codes because finding Allure is like trying to find the Bat Cave. The only way you knew about it was if you were invited there. I also installed a few in her room to see exactly what she was doing with them. I mean, if she was just talking to them that was still a violation, but if she was having sex with them and getting paid then she owed me money.

I would observe her for a couple of weeks before busting her ass because I wanted solid footage to show Earl, but in the meantime it would be on. I would only be giving her my nastiest, kinkiest clients. I'm talking about clients that even Holly would turn down, and she loved S&M clients. By the time I was done with her I would have her begging to be back at that dusty-ass strip club Earl dragged her up out of.

Simon, a client Earl introduced to Allure years ago, always had a thing for Kimona, but she would always deny his visits, saying that he was into shit that she wasn't. We had a room that was made up of nothing but mirrors on the walls and ceilings so you could watch yourself perform at every angle. He enjoyed the room because he was double jointed and could watch himself giving himself head. But while he was doing that, he wanted the girl that he was with to penetrate him anally so he could cum faster. After his ejaculation, he would lick it up himself and would want to kiss until he got up again. That was his request for the day, but sometimes it got even wilder than that. I remember one time he came in and said he wanted a girl to literally shit on him before they had sex like Biggie Smalls said on his *Ready to Die* CD.

He requested Kimona then too, and she declined, but since the day Earl came to visit a few weeks ago I'd been introducing her clients to the other girls in the house, letting them know that she wouldn't be here much longer. So if she wanted to make money, she had no choice but to take what I gave her. I even stopped calling her in for lineups if she wasn't already up there, to prove to her how I could get at her.

Simon looked like a Pee-wee Herman clone, complete with dork suit and bowtie. He would sometimes ask for girls to take home, but he looked like the type who would accidentally choke someone to death and go too far outside of a controlled setting, so we always told him no. He liked to already be in the room and naked when the girl got there, and always pretended to be a scared child when she walked in.

After we got him set up I called Kimona to the desk to service him. Of course she came with all kinds of attitude, and that just made me crack the hell up more on the inside because I knew what she was walking into.

As a rule, once you accepted the client and walked into the room, you were stuck with that client for the allotted time. She was mad because she couldn't understand why her clients hadn't been back to see her, not knowing that I was passing them off to the other girls. These bitches were cutthroat, so I wasn't worried about any of them saying anything, because most of them didn't like her anyway.

"Kimona, your client is waiting for you in the reflection room. Sign here for the assignment," I said to her, pushing over the printed receipt that showed that the client had paid for services. This receipt was printed once the client checked in for service, and was signed by the working girl to add to her tab for the night. Once you signed it, that was your client, and just as I figured, she didn't even ask to see who she was working with.

She signed her name with an attitude and pushed the paper back across the desk, causing the pen to fall to the floor. I didn't even bother to look up, because I knew I was about to get her ass back. She walked over to the bar to get a drink, I guess to get her groove right, but she would need more than a shot of Alizé to deal with Simon.

Brandy took the liberty of installing one of the cameras that we took from Kimona's apartment in a glass vase that decorated the room. The vase was already a decoration in that room, so it wasn't anything out of the ordinary that would have her feeling suspicious. I called Brandy from the back so she could watch what was going on too, and we had a good time laughing at the situation in front of us.

When Kimona walked into the room I could see her cringe a little because she had met Simon before, but she kept it professional and did what she went in there to do. Downing her drink in one gulp, she slammed her glass on the dresser, causing Simon to jump, but it excited him at the same time. He was completely naked, stretched out on the bed with his still-growing dick pointing toward the ceiling. This dude was nasty, and I was interested in seeing how Kimona was going to handle it, if she was going to control the situation or vice versa.

Stepping up on the bed, she stood over him with her legs resting on either side of his waist. The one thing we didn't have was sound, and I was so mad that I couldn't hear what they were saying. The two exchanged words then Kimona suddenly reached down and slapped him across the face with so much force, I was almost certain she left a handprint. She then squatted down so her knees were folded up into her chest, and Simon pulled her thong to the side and began finger-fucking her. She was stroking his dick with her free hand, using her other hand to balance herself on the bed in the stilettos she wore. He looked like he was losing it, and when he went to reach up and grab her breasts, she smacked him in his face again.

Pulling her shirt over her head, she put it around his neck, and after getting a good grip she pulled him up so that they were face to face. His facial expression looked like he was scared and excited at the same time, and whatever she was saying to him he agreed with it before she forcefully pushed him back on to the bed.

Simon brought his own strap-on every time he came because that was the one he liked to use and didn't want anything bigger or smaller than what he had. Although we had an on-site store that covered every fetish imaginable, he preferred his own shit. Simon helped her attach the strap-on to her body and began pulling other stuff out of his bag for them to use. She placed a bondage gag into his mouth that had a mask connected to it that covered his eyes and reins that connected to the back to control his head movement. I couldn't really see what the small box was that hung from the strap-on, but once Kimona started pushing buttons it came to life and started vibrating.

"Yo, he has a vibrating strap-on. As if anal penetration wasn't enough," I said to Brandy, both of us not believing our eyes.

I guess Simon figured since he was paying his hard-earned money, he might as well get his money's worth. Never mind this man was one of the top stock sellers in the DC area, he had a fetish that he loved to have fed.

Kimona wasn't even gentle with it. After applying a generous amount of lubrication to the dildo that was attached to her, she made him get up on the side of the bed with his ass up in the air, and rammed into him, pulling his head back with the reins from the mask.

I had to turn my head away for the second because I just knew he was going to hit the floor. To both my and Brandy's surprise he was throwing his ass back like he knew he was being taped, and I knew his face was red because of the shade of red his neck was turning.

"I know she better not kill his ass because today will be her last damn day." Brandy sipped on her drink, her face frowned up. We'd had an incident before where a client almost died, and Earl was pissed, so we tried to keep that kind of situation to a minimum.

Grabbing hold of his shoulders and letting go of the reins, she got up on his back like he was giving her a piggyback ride and pushed the strap-on in as far as it could go, causing Simon to buck back, throwing Kimona off his back. Brandy and I sat with our eyes glued to the screen like we were watching a movie, dying to see what was going to happen next.

Simon turned around and snatched the mask off his face, giving Kimona a look of death.

For the first time since she stepped in to the room, her face registered fear for a split second, but we trained our girls well. You had to know how to handle yourself in a situation if it got out of control, and if your aggressor knew you were scared, it could turn ugly quickly.

Simon approached Kimona in a menacing manner, but

she held her ground while she looked up at him from the floor. Dropping down in front of her, he grabbed her legs and pulled her up to him, making her lie flat on the cold, tiled floor. Not bothering to remove the dildo, he spread her legs to uncomfortable lengths and rammed into her, mercilessly making the dildo bounce against his stomach.

I knew there was going to be a problem because he didn't put on a condom and we don't play those games around these parts. I would have to suspend his membership for a while, but I wanted her to suffer, so I didn't go and break it up right away.

He bent down at the waist and started to deep-throat the dildo, but he kept pounding into her like he had a point to prove. With one hand he had her pinned down by her throat on to the floor and it looked like she was really gagging. Simon lifted back up and tightened the grip on her neck, and that's when I knew we had to go break it up.

"Brandy, go in the room with Desire and break up that session before he kills her ass, and make it quick. I don't feel like having to explain shit to Earl."

Brandy looked at me like she didn't care whether Kimona lived or not, but the look I returned made her hustle upstairs to the room because her ass would be under the ax too if something went down.

Watching her actions through the screen, I could see Brandy walking into the room just in time. Simon jumped back off of Kimona and scurried over to a corner like a frightened child. There was blood on the floor where Kimona lay gagging and choking on the floor. At that point I was shocked because I never wanted things to go that far. Brandy must have given him directions to get dressed and leave because I saw Desire and Brandy picking Kimona up from the floor and helping her out of the room.

I took that opportunity to get ghost after dismantling the display we had set up, because I didn't want Kimona to see me as they walked by. Hopefully the bitch learned a lesson from it, but I had more shit in store for her ass. I wanted her to be so fed up she would just leave, and now was just the beginning.

The Evidence

A week after that incident with Kimona and Simon, I went to retrieve the cameras from her place while she was down at the gynecologist for a follow-up visit. Come to find out, when we thought he was having vaginal sex with her he actually penetrated her anally and ripped a lot of tissue, which caused the bleeding. I felt bad at first, but the doctor said it wasn't that bad, that she had to be on bed rest for a few weeks to get her self together. When I explained her situation to Earl he went the hell off, coming back to Allure several days in a row to check on Kimona and to put Brandy and I in place.

I still wanted her ass out, though, so it didn't matter. I took the footage I had from the camera outside of her door first to see exactly who she had coming in and out. Just as I suspected, she had some of the guys she serviced at Allure coming to her crib, and a few of them were men I'd never seen before coming through for a hook-up. I switched to the tape in the living room, and then to the bedroom. It appeared that she would entertain in the living room, and when they went into the bedroom the guy would put money in her nightstand drawer before they handled business. Just as I thought, the bitch was stealing.

Knowing what I did, I had to use her until the very end when I showed Earl the tape. He was pissed about what we did to her and that was cool, but when he saw that his precious little Kimona was taking money off the top he'd change his mind. I was sure of it. In the meantime I had two more guys to interview for positions before I went to Earl with my proposal.

The way I figured it was that we could split the house up a little. We had set times that men showed up for an appointment, so the times in between we could use for the women. I also figured that women could be invited from the same clubs and seminars that he invited the men from. Everything seemed to be falling into place, and when my third interviewee showed up, I was convinced that it could be pulled off.

Finesse was the bomb. An extra dark chocolate hunk of a man, he stood about six feet, three inches tall and looked like an African warrior. He had muscles EVERYWHERE, and I started to salivate just looking at him. Brandy was at a loss for words also, and we were shocked when he popped a CD into the stereo system that was on the wall and began dancing like we were still at the club. As Lil Jon was screaming "OK!" he was popping it like he was in the video. I mean, he actually showed up in a costume, complete with pull-away pants, and was greased up and everything. For the first time I didn't think I liked what I saw until the music slowed down and he came and plucked Brandy from her seat, spreading her out on the floor in front of my desk.

J. Holiday was singing about putting us to bed, and Finesse had Brandy laid down like he intended on fucking her right to sleep. I stood up so I could see what he was really doing, and he had her in a sixty-nine position, his dick dangling in her face and his face between her legs, acting like he was eating her out through her clothes. This dude really thought he was at a show or something, and for a second I almost tucked a dollar in his G-string.

Feeding into the show, I started pumping him up so I could see some meat. I wanted to know if he was stuffing his G-string or if he was really working with some shit.

He got up off her and was gyrating to the music as he stepped out the rest of his costume and stood before us completely naked. I, for one, was happy with what I saw, but I knew that I couldn't hire him because, although clients paid for a show, that was too much of a show. What he did was more for the club and private parties. My clients paid for sex, and most of them didn't feel like all that.

I wasn't a fool, though. He wouldn't be leaving until I got a piece of him myself because a big dick didn't guarantee a good stroke. Once I saw what he was working with, I thought just maybe if I talked to him and told him what we did here, he could get it right. I would just have to see.

Taking a seat on the side of my desk, I watched him remove Brandy's thong with his teeth, a skill that most didn't possess. He wasted no time devouring her in front of me. Every time Brandy would scoot back he would scoot up, not letting go of her clit. I thought they were going to make a complete circle because they started out in front of my desk, and by the time he got finished, she was by the door. He was tossing her around like she was a rag doll, and I started to change my mind a little about keeping him around.

Standing up on his feet, he pulled her up by her waist so she was hanging upside down in the sixty-nine position. He walked back and forth in front of my desk, eating her pussy while she held onto his legs and sucked his dick. This dude was a beast, and I'd never seen nothing like it up close and personal.

As he walked back toward the wall, he turned her body right-side up and pinned her to the wall. I don't know where he pulled the condom from, but he managed to balance her body against the wall and slide the condom on before dicking her down, and I was truly impressed. The muscles in his back were ripped and flexing from him pounding the hell out of Brandy, and I wanted in on the action.

His legs were spread, so I took the liberty of massaging his balls and kissing him up and down his back. I wanted him to save some for me before he came. Brandy had her legs locked around him so tight he had to pry them off. That dick must have been damn good. Once she got down I pulled the condom he had on off, and replaced it with a ribbed Magnum from my private stash. Brandy's my girl and all that, but not like that to be exchanging bodily fluid.

Just as we were about to get into it, the desk phone began to ring. All of us froze completely and looked at the pink phone like it was a foreign object. It rang a couple of times before I motioned for Brandy to answer it. The look on her face did not register well, and my stomach started to turn.

I motioned for Finesse to put me down, and by then his dick had gone limp, so that was the end of it anyway.

I was trying to "ear-hustle" on the conversation by standing closer to Brandy, and my eyes bugged out when

I heard Earl's voice on the other end. Apparently he was close to the establishment and wanted to have a meeting with Brandy and I about what happened with Kimona, since we never really got a chance to talk about it. Shit was about to hit the fan, but more importantly, I had to get Finesse out of my office.

We went into speed mode, getting Finesse dressed in record time and lighting candles while we put my office back in order. I hustled Finesse down the hallway and on to the elevator, letting him know that we would finish up what we started at a later date.

Rushing back to my office, I used the sink in the adjoining bathroom to wash off the grease from Finesse's oily body and changed into a pair of sweat pants and a wife beater. I opened my laptop and uploaded the video from the tapes I'd pulled from Kimona's apartment just in case I had to use them. Something was telling me that bitch was trying to get me up out of here, but shit wouldn't be that easy.

Brandy went to check the books and supplies in the lab and at the bar after removing the camera from the reflection room, just in case Earl decided to look around.

When he walked into my office, I had my glasses on and was typing away at absolutely nothing, just to look busy. I gave him a bright smile when the door opened, but he didn't return it. That's when I knew it was going to be a problem.

"Hey, Earl, what brings you to this neck of the woods this evening?" I asked, a curious look on my face.

"Well, to be up front with you, I don't like the things I've been hearing lately. Have you been giving Kimona's clients to the other girls? What's the mix-up?"

"Kimona has been stealing from Allure. We discussed

that the last time you were here. Now, I'll admit that I've been making things hard on her, but if I let these girls start slipping and getting away with stuff, they'll walk all over me. You're trusting me to run a business, and that's what I'm doing."

I was pissed. I was so tired of talking about this Kimona shit. The girl was a damn thief, and back in the day thieves got their damn hands cut off. Something was telling me there was more to it with him and Kimona, but like I explained to her when she first got here, Earl was a married man. He had a wife and kids at home, and if he cared that much about her, why would he have her working in a whorehouse? If she was that important, why wasn't she sitting up somewhere living it up? Things that make you go, *hmmm.*

"Dee, I understand all that, and I feel what you're saying. You have a business to run, I got that. But when the workers are not happy, money is not getting made at its fullest potential."

"You make a good point," I replied, not giving him more than that. I'd been running this shit for the past six years, and it wasn't until recently that Kimona's books started coming up short, and what was I supposed to do in that case? If it were anyone else, they would have been got the boot.

"All I'm saying is, give the girl a chance to redeem herself. Why would you send her in the room with Simon, knowing what kind of person he is? Holly usually handles him, and we've never had an incident like that with her. What are you trying to prove?"

"I don't have anything to prove. She's the thief. I just need her to recognize who's in charge here."

"Dee, me and you are here," he said, giving me eye

contact and using his fingers to point that out. "I trust you to do what you do, but you have to be a little more trusting of your girls."

"Look, I want you to see something," I said to him as I turned my laptop around to face him. This was the kind of shit that I needed him to understand that made my job hard.

"What is this?" he asked as he scooted closer to the screen.

"This is what Kimona doesn't tell you."

I let the tape play and speak for itself. Earl was well aware of the rules, because he made them, so the things that he was witnessing were way out of the box. Kimona knew she shouldn't have men in her apartment, and that if she wanted to entertain she had to get her own shit somewhere else and give her spot up to someone who really wanted it.

His face went through so many emotions as he watched his prized possession break every rule in the book. This shit was going to be hilarious because it's not like I just went around picking on people; you had to give me a reason to bring stress your way, and Kimona definitely stressed me the hell out.

"How long has this been going on?" he asked with disbelief in his voice. Streaming video doesn't lie, and he had it all right in his face,

"Torri told me about it months ago, but this video is from about a month ago."

"OK, continue things the way you have. But, Dee," he said, practically pleading with me, "please, just give her a break. I think putting her in there with Simon has taught her a lesson. Let her start from scratch, and I'll just take the loss on what she owes, OK?"

"OK, Earl, but what does that say about how we run things if she keeps getting away with shit?"

"I'll talk to her. Just one more chance, OK?"

"I'll trust you on this, but if your girl doesn't shape up, I'll have to ship her out. I have no choice, if I'm going to maintain control around here."

He didn't bother to respond, he just got up and walked out of the office. Once my door was shut I breathed a sigh of relief because in reality I needed to get my shit together as well. Making sure to save the video of Kimona to my files, I closed my laptop and leaned my seat back. I would give her another chance, but this was it. Kimona better walk a straight line or she'd be walking a line back to the damn strip club.

The Plan

Kimona took an extra two weeks to get her shit together, but her stink attitude had gotten worse. I figured some of her brain cells must have been destroyed during the incident with Simon because she had the snaps and was acting like she really didn't want to be here. My thing is, if you don't like it here, beat your feet. No one was holding her hostage.

I started sending a few of her clients back her way, and from what they reported, she was performing at top capacity. Just to mix it up I always threw a client of Holly's in there, as a reminder that I was the Queen Bitch around here.

Earl stopped by a couple more times, but eventually his visits dwindled back down to nothing, just as before. A part of me was thinking that maybe he and Kimona were creeping around, but I would never ask him about it. She was just working her way out the door slowly but surely.

Among other things, I was getting closer to convincing

Earl to let the guys in. As a test run I brought in Hot Chocolate to service a woman I met at the mayor's dinner with Earl a while back. She was pretty and slim and had a slight attitude, which I chalked up to her not getting good sex at home.

I approached her discreetly while she was sitting at her table by herself. Her husband was on the other side of the room all in this young girl's face, and she didn't look like she was having fun at all. Like she was forced to be there. I studied her for a while to gauge how I would approach her after watching her turn away one person after another. I was a little hesitant, but after I got my nerve up and got it in my head what I was going to say, it was on.

"You're Mayor Gibson's wife, correct?" I asked as I slid in the seat next to her. She was a little hesitant to answer at first, but I'm a girl who always gets what I want, so that wasn't a deterrent. I knew what I had to do.

"Yes, I am. And you are?" she asked with a snide attitude.

I knew I would have to play it gentle with her if I was going to get her to follow my lead. "Dee," I responded, giving her a warm smile. Surprisingly she returned it. "Are you enjoying the festivities this evening?"

"These things are boring. I'm forced to be here to support my husband, although that bitch that he's been following around all night doesn't seem to know I'm present."

I knew exactly who she was talking about because she'd made it easier for me to pick my target. What the mayor's wife didn't know was that bitch she was mad at was a girl from Allure that the mayor had been seeing for a while.

"Does that bother you? Seeing your husband with that woman in front of your face?"

"Of course, it does," she said with nervous laughter. "But I've learned to make due. After all, he does make sure I maintain a lavish lifestyle."

"I feel you on that." I laughed along with her, seeing the ice between us melt into a puddle. "Well, what do you do for satisfaction?"

"Satisfaction?" she asked like she was clueless and didn't know what the word meant.

"Yes, satisfaction. How do you scratch that itch that I'm sure your husband hasn't scratched in ages?"

The look on her face said everything, and I knew I had her at that point. If she was willing to drop a couple thousand on a Louis Vuitton, why not drop it on something that gave you that same satisfaction that would possibly hold you over for a couple days?

"Well, it's been a while since any . . . *itch* of that nature has been scratched. What are you proposing?" she asked, leaning into me so that we could talk without everyone being in our business.

At that moment I took the opportunity to pitch Allure to her.

She listened intently as I explained the workings of Allure and how discreet we operated so that she wouldn't have to worry about her husband finding out. The only issue I would have was keeping her out of sight of the girl who was here with the mayor now, but since it would be her first time, I would take her straight to the room where she would be serviced.

By the end of that night I had her credit card information and a date set in my planner to put into the computer when I got back. That was why I had to go into finding men to work at the spot. I knew if the mayor's wife liked how we did business at Allure, she would bring in some friends, and so on. Allure would be popping in no time, and Earl would love me for it.

I had the mayor's wife coming in at nine, and once she described to me what she was looking for, I knew Hot Chocolate would be perfect for her. Taking the liberty of planting a camera in the Plush Room, I had Hot Chocolate already situated for her when she came in.

She showed up dressed like she was going to pull a heist, in all black and big Jackie O shades, that made me laugh.

After swiping her card and checking the platinum bracelet on her wrist, I escorted her up to her room personally. When I opened the door, Hot Chocolate had the room lit by candlelight, and there were soft plush pillows strategically placed throughout the space. The colors in the room ranged from deep maroon to blood red, and I could smell the strawberry candles that were placed around as well.

The smile that was on her face as she stepped into the room said everything, and when I passed her over to Hot Chocolate, I knew she was going to be a happy camper.

I raced back downstairs and I turned on the monitor in my office so I could watch how he handled her. He handled me quiet well, so I knew she was going to be cool.

He wasted no time getting her situated and removing her clothes. She had a nice, petite frame, but her breasts were definitely paid for. Hot Chocolate started with a sensual massage with scented oils to help her relax, and at that point she was down to her thong. The rest of her clothes were neatly stacked in the corner on top of her purse.

He was completely naked and standing at attention, but he took his time relaxing her and heating up the situation. Now, she'd said she wanted the ultimate pleasure and anything went, so I knew Hot Chocolate was going to turn up the heat pretty soon. If what he did to me was just for the interview, I knew he was going to put it down.

I turned from the monitor to take a quick call, and surprisingly it was the mayor requesting an urgent visit to see Torri within the next hour. He said that since his wife was out of town he wanted to come get off while she was away. I laughed inside because if the mayor's wife was going to continue to creep out, she was going to have to get her lies together.

We talked for a minute while I tried to see how I could get the mayor in and get the wife out without them running into each other.

The way I figured it, the mayor's wife wouldn't want to be seen in here, so she wouldn't be stopping by the bar to get drinks or anything like that. The mayor had the tendency to be a bit of a social butterfly, so if I could get him to come after she left or while she was still fully occupied with Hot Chocolate, I'd be good.

"Well, sir, Torri won't actually be free until about eleven-thirty, so I can give you that slot. If you want, you can come about fifteen minutes early and relax a little in the lounge to wait for her. The jungle room is open, so you can relax in there and wait for her also."

Thankfully he agreed to it, and I called Torri up right away to let her know I wanted her in the room waiting for the mayor when he got here at eleven-fifteen. I just had to let Hot Chocolate know I needed him to keep the wife occupied long enough for me to get her husband into the Jungle Room, which was right across the hall from where she was.

Turning back to the screen, I was happy that I was able to install a small microphone in the room so that I could hear what was going on as well. Hot Chocolate was laid back on some throw pillows on the floor, and he had the mayor's wife, completely naked and on her knees, deep-throating him while he held on to the bun on the back of her head..

I needed them to get to having sex soon, because when trying to be sneaky, time always snuck up on you, and I wanted her to be satisfied completely, so she could bring her friends back. The thing was, the men had to be on call for now until I got things situated with Earl, so I would definitely have to make appointments. Once the clients' cards were charged, though, it was non-refundable. So either they showed up and got their money's worth or they lost out.

I was happy to see that the wife had tricks of her own, placing the condom inside of her mouth and sliding it down on Hot Chocolate's dick like she'd been doing it all her life. It briefly made me wonder why her sex life was so dry with the mayor, since they both seemed like freaks, but maybe they were together for convenience.

Right on schedule, the mayor's wife moved up and straddled Hot Chocolate and began riding him like a pro, their moans turning me the hell on. I was so into it, I reached down into my pants and spread the lips of my pussy so that I could finger myself. I few tugs on my clit ring had me amped up, and I had to stifle a few moans myself so I could pay attention to the clock.

Hot Chocolate was blessed with length and width, so I know she was having a damn ball bouncing up and down on him.

Come to find out, the wife was pretty flexible too. She went from a squatting position to sitting down on his dick and throwing her legs over his shoulders, balancing her weight out on her arms as she continued to bounce up and down on him and he used a bullet on her clit at high speed.

I was pulling on my clit ring harder and faster as I was nearing an explosion, but a quick glance at the clock set me back because the mayor would be arriving in a matter of minutes.

I sent Hot Chocolate a quick message to the Bluetooth he was wearing, letting him know to keep her occupied until at least eleven forty-five, giving me enough time to get the mayor in the room and situated.

I met him at the elevator and took his card from him while we walked right up to his room. To my surprise, both Torri and Kimona were naked and waiting on him. I looked at Torri for an answer but couldn't really get into it because the client was already there. I was puzzled, though, because I thought they hated each other, but it seemed as though they were trying to play me. Kimona was already on my list, and I hoped I wouldn't have to get rid of Torri as well.

When I got back to the desk I checked the mayor in and tucked his card inside an envelope for him until he came back out.

A few minutes later his wife, escorted by Hot Chocolate, was coming down the stairs, and she had a very satisfied look on her face. I smiled at her as she was escorted to the elevator. I knew I had that one in the bag. It was just a matter of time before she started sending her people my way, and I couldn't wait.

As for Kimona, I would handle her and Torri's conniving asses accordingly.

The Snitch

I pulled Torri into the office a few days later to dig in her ass about that shit she pulled with Kimona and the mayor. "Torri, what was that shit with you and Kimona the other day? When did y'all become all buddy buddy?"

She looked hesitant to reply, but the look on my face said that I was not joking. How in hell were the house snitch and the house bitch going to try and play me? I'd have both their asses up and out this joint so fast they'd have to question if they ever worked here.

"She told me that you sent her up there," Torri replied like she didn't really want to say.

"I sent her up there? Why would I do that? The mayor didn't ask for a threesome," I responded in shock. Kimona was working my nerves, and I had just the thing to get her back. I couldn't wait for the day to come when I could pack her shit and set her on the curb.

She continued to tell me how she was preparing the room for the mayor by lighting candles and making sure there were fresh fruit and syrups for him because he liked to get sticky while having sex. She was watching the clock to make sure she was on point when Kimona walked in and told her she was sent up there by me. When Torri said that she was going to call me to confirm, Kimona told her that I was busy entertaining at the bar and didn't want to be bothered.

I was pissed because on that night when I checked the slips for the lab I had one for the mayor's room that confused me, but I didn't question it, thinking maybe the mayor had gotten the pills for Torri. It never crossed my mind that Kimona would have gotten them, and I knew they weren't for the mayor because, being in politics, he had to stay clean at all times.

The report I got from the lab showed that Kimona had gone back to get pills twice, and I briefly wondered if she was selling them on the outside. I mean, was the girl strung out or what? We had an in-house therapist that she could see if she needed to stretch out on the couch, but doing vindictive shit did not make me sympathize with you. She should have come to me when the problem first began.

This was the kind of shit that I was trying to tell Earl about her. She was just doing simple shit, but I had something for her ass.

I met this guy at Club Destiny who was into some real weird shit, like sticking peeled bananas in his ass and shit like that, and I made sure I sent him to Kimona when he finally stopped by. I know that Earl said to stop giving her S&M clients, but this bitch just didn't seem to get the picture. You can't just do what you want to do around these parts. There were rules and order to everything, but she was insistent on going against the grain, so she would get the hand I dealt her. She was getting up out this joint, if it was the last thing I did, but not before I put her ass in one last situation that she'd never forget. She would definitely hate me after this, and that's was exactly the way I wanted it.

I called Brandy to the office. I broke it down for her and had Torri repeat the situation from the other day when the mayor was here. Now, just to give credit where it was due, the mayor had no complaints about the two of them being in there, and he enjoyed himself so much that he left a nice healthy tip for them at the door while he waited on his driver to circle around the block. I gave the entire tip to Torri, not bothering to break Kimona off with any of it because she was being sneaky and didn't deserve it. She had a quota to meet if she wanted to stay here, though, and I wasn't cutting her any shorts.

I spoke to Holly about some of her freakiest, nastiest clients, and she had the perfect guy for me that was guaranteed to run Kimona out of here for good. Of course she introduced me to George, an Internet success who made millions after his website, MyFreakSpace, took off a few years ago. He had all kinds of money that he didn't mind spending, as long as you were compliant with what he wanted during a session.

I had to show Kimona that I wasn't playing, and at that point I didn't care what Earl had to say. She had been nothing but trouble since she'd been here, and I wanted her out. George had a kinky fetish that was so over-the-top, it was ridiculous, and I knew it would be something that Kimona wouldn't be able to handle. Since it was the last day of the month she had to at least do George to make her quota or she would get the boot, and I had been purposely not sending her a lot of clients, just so she could fall short. The downside to that was if she went ahead with what George wanted, I would have to have her around for another month, but I would definitely be letting Earl know that she was stealing again.

I asked Holly if she minded if I talked to George. I wanted him to turn it up a notch when Kimona was in there with him. I didn't want him to choke her or try to rape and kill her, but I wanted this session to be one for the books. I wanted it extra nasty and degrading, and I knew he would be able to pull it off without a hitch.

George was happy to comply, and I gave him a nice discount on his service for the night because he was doing me a huge favor.

I was definitely setting up a camera and microphone in that room. As always, I had to have the last laugh. I thought about totally humiliating her and putting all of the footage I had on tape and selling it, but that would be putting Allure out there, and Earl would have a fit.

I dismissed Torri shortly after letting her know that she had something to prove too before her ass got the boot. Just as she was leaving I received a call from the mayor's wife looking to book an appointment. Two of her girlfriends wanted to come by as well, and that was perfect, because I could put all three to work.

I knew this would work out, and once I showed Earl what kind of money I had made off of it he wouldn't have a choice but to let me move forward. I was planning to do this for about a month just to see what kind of money I could make in a thirty-day period, and since the mayor's wife was willing to spread the word, I knew I would have the clientele to keep making it do what it do.

The good thing is, the men didn't live onsite, so he wouldn't have to worry about room and board for them, but eventually the same rules would apply and they would be housed here as well. The men had day jobs, though, with two of them doing construction and the last one owning a barbershop, so I didn't want to pull them out of their element just in case it dried up for them. Men would always pay for sex, but when we're moody, it could change at any minute, and I wanted the guys to still be able to make their money.

I didn't even bother to call Kimona into my office because I didn't feel like hearing her practiced excuses. She always had a reason why she did the stupid shit she did, but it would be over soon. I couldn't wait! I smiled through the rest of my day, just knowing that things would finally be going in my favor.

For our end-of-the-month meeting I called all of the girls to the round table to let everyone know what was really going on. I didn't like surprises, so I let the women know the day before the end of the month every month who had made their quota already, who didn't, and what they had to do to make it happen. That way, when they shit got packed up the next night there weren't any surprises. Also, the girl who made the most for the month by the end of the next night got a bonus added to her pay, whether it was a free spa day or extra money. Kimona usually walked away with the winnings every month, but lately she'd been slipping and everyone knew it.

I didn't bring the men into the meeting because I didn't want the girls to know that I had already set that plan into motion and that I was already making money off of it. Bitches talk, and I didn't need shit getting back to Earl too soon.

I was happy with the way things were going, and Brandy seemed cool with it too. I thought her and Finesse had been seeing each other, but I wasn't sure. You know there aren't any secrets around here, and one of the girls asked me what was up with Brandy lately. She's been stuck ever since he came here, but I had to set some things into action before I could worry about other stuff.

"OK, ladies, now that we are up to speed, does anyone have any questions or concerns?" I looked around the room at all of the women, and it was sad because, come tomorrow night, if that money wasn't right they'd be getting their last check on the way out the door. "Well, ladies, that's all I have to say. Let's hope we survive the weekend."

I quickly gathered my papers from the podium and exited the room, but not before peeping the sour face Kimona wore. She knew it was a setup, and she knew she had to at least do one client to make her quota, but I wouldn't be calling her for any lineups. I would let her know that George had arrived and that was it. Now, if she was a smart whore she'd wait around the bar so that if I did a lineup she'd know, but I knew Kimona, and that wasn't her thing, so it would be on.

I whistled as I walked back down to my office. I made a few calls to line up some stuff for next week with some clients I hadn't seen around in a while, and even offered a few discounts to those who'd been coming on the regular, to get them in. They usually made up the difference in drinks and drugs at the bar, so I wasn't worried about it. Tomorrow couldn't get there fast enough, and for once I was happy about the way things were turning out.

I returned a couple of calls and made sure the liquor order was filled so the bar could be stocked for the next thirty days. Everything was going as planned, and I couldn't wait to see it all in action.

I willed the hours to speed by as I updated files and spreadsheets before I sat back and watched the session with Hot Chocolate and the mayor's wife again. Once I saw how she interacted in the group session she booked, I'd know whether I wanted to get a taste of her myself.

The senator was starting to buzz around again for Holly as well, which was good news for her because she currently held the top spot, with Torri in at a close second. The competition was looking good, and I liked that the girls felt like they had to hustle to stay around. That way hopefully they'd never let their guard down.

I finally went to lay down after the last client was in for their appointment, and I would be up again early in the morning to make sure all the money was collected and the house was clear. Then it would be show time.

The Big Payback

Starting in the early afternoon a lot of men were coming through to spend their paycheck on their favorite working girl. These same men who had families at home showed up like clockwork to pay homage to the power of pussy. It was ridiculous, but it made Earl a very rich man, so I wasn't mad.

Just as I thought, the lineups were popping off all evening, but Kimona didn't make herself available for any of them. I made her aware that she had a ten o'clock appointment scheduled, and I let her know how much it paid, so she would know if she did it she'd make her quota. She took the bait, of course, and that made me smile the rest of the day.

I had the mayor's wife and the two friends she brought along set up with my three men in the ice room all together because they wanted a group sex session and didn't complain when I charged them twice the amount of the normal group rate.

My top girls had clients back to back, and my lineup was getting smaller and smaller as clients came in all evening to pay for services. The lab was threatening to run out of ecstasy, and the bar was popping all night. It was getting closer and closer to the time for Kimona to meet up with George, and I couldn't contain my excitement.

By seven o'clock Torri and Holly were still running neck and neck and were killing the lineup, giving each client exactly two hours and then putting them to the side. A good amount of men asked for Kimona, and she could have really come up, but she wasn't available, and I damn sure wasn't going to look for her. If you want money, come make it, and if you don't, stay where you at. A lot of the men hung around at the bar and lounge area to wind down after they were serviced, and a couple of them paid again to be with a different girl for another session. I don't even ask questions, I just take the money and keep it moving.

Around eight-thirty Kimona decided to show her face, and the men in the lounge went wild. The thing is, it didn't matter, because the clients were serviced for two hours and she had an appointment at ten. That brought a lot of disappointment to the room, but if she made her quota she'd at least be there the next day to get paid.

I watched her walk around and flirt with the customers, a few tucking money in the waist of the extra-short shorts she was wearing, and in the straps of her sandals that laced all the way up to the thigh.

Kimona was a simple bitch, I swear. She had people paying her and she wasn't even performing a service. Every chick that worked here wanted that kind of power, but she walked around like it was supposed to be that way. That was part of the reason why we didn't get along. She didn't believe her shit stunk, but I was going to be the one who smeared it in her damn face so she could smell if for herself. She was an attractive woman with so much potential, but her attitude just made it so hard to like her, and I was past the point where I was trying to make it work.

I remember when Earl first brought her here. She was so humble then. I was just promoted from working girl to madam, although I was still turning tricks here and there. Earl used to be my daddy when I was a streetwalker, but when he got the space that we now call Allure, I made sure to bring the only woman who had my back out there with me. Brandy and I made lots of money together, and I didn't see why it had to stop.

After three short years, Allure went from just working weekends and Brandy and I still having to walk the strip to the most happening underground spot in the metropolitan DC area, and a multi-million dollar business. We'd come a long way, and I was certainly not letting one immature little girl who wanted to throw tantrums ruin it all. I never thought I'd see the day when I would have to be this way with Kimona, but it was about that time, and I had to do what I had to do.

At nine forty-five George showed up, his platinum bracelet blinging against his all-black ensemble and a fresh cut. He didn't look half as kinky as I knew he would be, and I knew that would throw Kimona off track. I took his pass from him and walked him over to the bar so he could get right. He requested ecstasy pills from the gate, so I personally went to the lab and threw in a few extra ones, so he could be good and horny.

I made sure he had downed his first drink and popped two of his pills before I brought Kimona over to introduce the two. I could see from the look in her eyes that she liked what she saw, but this dude was a Doctor Jekyll and Mr. Hyde, and she would feel differently once they were alone.

I wanted to keep her at the bar, so I brought the slips over for her to sign, and once again she didn't even bother to read them before signing. Everything was going too well, and I was looking for something to go wrong, but surprisingly things were running smooth.

I went to let Kimona know that it was ten o'clock, and that meant it was time to take her client to be serviced. I did another lineup because there were about nine girls who still weren't working, and we needed to get as much money in as possible before the books closed at one AM for the day. I always did one o'clock instead of midnight, so the girls could at least get an eleven o'clock client and still get paid for the day before.

Once everyone was settled and the bar had a chance to re-stock, I took my seat in the office and turned on the monitor so I could watch Kimona and George in action. I knew at first he would be gentle with her like they were going to have normal everyday sex, but he'd definitely flip the script on her ass in due time, and I needed to see it all go down. This was the satisfaction I was waiting for, and if she forfeited the client she wouldn't make her quota. I couldn't sit still because I was so excited, and the best part was neither one of then knew the camera was in there.

Taking a sip of my drink, I sat back to enjoy the show. Two hours from now I'd have my revenge.

PART TWO

Kimona

BY BRITTANI WILLIAMS

Kimona:

Playing Tricks

"Get on your knees, crawl to me, and get ready to blow!" Those were the first words the client spoke to me. I could see that he didn't waste any time. I hadn't gotten a full glimpse of his face, so I wasn't even sure who he was. I didn't really care; my goal was to make the quota for the night to buy me more time to put my plan into action. Dee thought she had me where she wanted me, but she was sadly mistaken. I would make her pay for all the shit she'd tried to pull the last few weeks, and victory would be in the air for me to grab hold of.

I got on my knees at the door and began crawling over to the spot where he was sitting. The dim lighting made it difficult to see his face, but the closer I got, the more the details were revealed. I recognized him as one of Holly's clients.

This bitch has tried to set me up again! I thought. I'd be damned if I was going to end up at the doctor again with my ass ripped to shreds, but I would try to make the best of this for the sake of buying more time. There he was, sitting in the black leather chair. His ass was almost to the end of the seat, and his legs were spread wide open. His fingers were tightly wrapped around his slowly growing member, and his free hand was motioning me to come closer.

"I need you to blow this dick like you've never done any dick before!" he ordered while stroking himself, causing it to grow a little more.

Giving head was something that I had mastered over the years, and I had never been with him before, so I was damn sure going to make him believe he was getting the royal treatment. He pointed his dick in my direction as I opened my mouth wide enough to fit it inside. I tried to reach up and grab hold of it, but he quickly slapped my hand away. So there I was, on all fours, bobbing my head back and forth on his hard dick. I could feel the pre-cum trickling down my throat as he began to move back and forth on the edge of the chair, forcing his dick deeper into my mouth.

"You like the taste of that?" he asked as I continued the motion.

I agreed by nodding my head in a quick motion before going back to work. For one of Holly's clients he was pretty calm, unlike the other client that damn near killed me. Giving him head was beginning to turn me on. His moans were making me wet the crotch of my panties as I moved back and forth. I was ready to jump on him the longer I put my jaw muscles to work. But he was running the show, so I would wait patiently until he was ready to fill me up.

A few minutes later he removed his member from my mouth so quickly that I couldn't catch the juices that dripped from my mouth, ran down my chin, and splattered on my breasts.

"Turn around and lean your back against this chair," he demanded in a tone that made my pussy pulsate even more.

I obeyed his command and anxiously awaited his next move.

"So, you like sucking dick, huh?"

"Yes," I quickly replied. I sat still, waiting.

He grabbed my chin to push my head back on the cushion of the chair where his ass was resting just a few minutes earlier. I figured he wanted more head so I opened wide. With force he shoved his hard dick down my throat, causing me to gag.

I tried to push him back, but he continued to move in and out of my mouth, hitting my tonsils each time. Tears were running down my cheeks, and I felt like I was just short of throwing up. I tried to push him away and was still unsuccessful.

"Am I hurting you, baby?" he asked, quickly changing his tone.

Now he wants to play sensitive? He knew good and damn well shoving his dick down someone's throat would hurt. I played his game, though, and nodded.

He got down on his knees and looked me in the eye. "I'm sorry, I get a little rough sometimes."

I sat there wondering what he would do next. I had learned over the years that most of the customers here were unpredictable. The best thing I could do was be prepared for anything.

He pulled me up from the floor, turned me around, and placed one of my legs up on the leather chair. My foot was comfortably resting on the cushion as I positioned both of my hands on the arms of the chair and pointed my ass in the air as far as I could get it. He stood back and stared at me while caressing his member, which was still rock-hard even after the brief intermission. I could hear him ripping open a condom wrapper and putting it on, but he still wasn't budging. Instead, he was still standing in the same spot watching me and jacking off.

Unexpectedly, he moved closer and rammed his dick inside of me. *I guess we're back to the rough shit,* I thought, but he slowed down his pace once he was inside and began to caress my ass. I didn't understand this guy; he must've had a crazy childhood or something because this split personality shit was ridiculous.

Soon his rhythm was feeling good to me, and I was able to relax for the first time since I'd entered the room. I could feel the tension building in my body as my tunnel created more juice than normal. I could soon feel the juices running out of me. He was slapping my ass and turning me on. I had actually forgotten about the fact that he had tried to choke me to death a few minutes earlier. I was enjoying it, and I'm sure he knew by the loud moans I generously let out.

He had the stamina of a horse and didn't stop even for a second to take a breath. I loved a man who knew how to keep it going. Even after I tightened my pussy muscles around his stick he didn't miss a beat. My thick ass continued to bounce as he pounded me from behind.

I wish he had shown this side a little bit earlier, because we could have had a lot more fun, or at least I could have. Strangely, I could tell that he enjoyed everything that he'd done since he'd been here.

"I want to bust in your face," he moaned loudly.

I didn't respond because I damn sure wasn't trying to let this nut spray cum all over my face.

"You hear me? I'm gonna bust all over that pretty little face of yours," he repeated.

My mood from went from satisfied to annoyed. I could

tell by his fast breathing that he was nearing an orgasm. I hoped he wouldn't be able to hold out long enough to turn me around, but I was fooled. He pulled out of me, ripped the condom off, and pushed me down in the chair. He climbed onto the arms, his dick hanging over my face, and pulsating as if it were about to explode. He looked me in the eye and I didn't say a word. I closed my eyes when he was about to blow and could soon feel his warm release dripping all over my face. I was afraid to open my eyes, so I waited.

He continued to beat his stick while moaning at the same time. "Get ready for this golden shower!" he said.

Before I had a chance to respond he was peeing all over my face. I could feel the hot liquid running off my chin and down my body. I was disgusted and I dared not open my mouth for fear that I would end up swallowing his body fluids. Once he got down off the chair I sat there like a mannequin until he passed me a towel to clean myself off.

"You're much better than Holly. I may have to pick you more often," he said, picking his clothing up from the floor and heading toward the bathroom.

I didn't say a word because there was no way in hell he would be seeing me again. I waited until he was done cleaning up and headed toward the door before I moved.

On his way out he had one more thing to say: "I'll leave you a hefty tip at the door. You were well worth it!"

After he left the room, I sat there for a few seconds. I knew that I had made my quota and I did what I had to do, but I had never felt so degraded the entire time I had been working at Allure. I gathered up what little clothing I had on before our session started and quickly got dressed.

As soon as I opened the door, Dee was standing there

with a grim look on her face. I was sure that she was pissed that her plan didn't work. There was no way I was going to go out that easy. I made it past the thirty-day probation; now I just had to get in good with Earl again to get her ass out of here.

"Why the grim look? Mad that I made my quota?" I asked, trying to piss her off even more.

"Don't think you're safe yet. I still have a few tricks up my sleeve," she replied, pointing her finger in my direction.

"That's the problem with you, you're working with tricks. Me, on the other hand, I'm working with skills! Trust me, I will come out on top," I said before brushing past her to leave the floor.

I wasn't going to let her see me sweat. I knew it wouldn't be easy to get back on Earl's good side after I'd betrayed him the way I had, but I was going to figure out a way to make it work. I had been doing a little research on Dee myself, and I knew about her having men working without Earl knowing. She hadn't even been giving him any of the money she was making while using his facility. I knew he wouldn't be happy about that, especially since she brought it to his attention and he hadn't approved it yet.

Torri was next on my list. I figured that if I got close to her, I could play my cards right. She definitely was competition for me in the house, but once I was running the show, competition wouldn't be an issue.

Running Allure had been my plan since day one, but Earl felt that I was too good of a moneymaker not to be in the lineup. I thought it was crazy, since he had told me time and time again that I would be the one running the house once it opened. Out of nowhere, things changed between us when Dee came along and I was forced to work in the house.

I'd heard rumors of their relationship, but I decided to let it go because she knew just as well as I did that Earl was a married man and definitely wasn't going to leave his wife for a working girl. It took me a long time to realize that, since I was always depending on a man to be around.

Growing up, all I had was myself. My mother was a prostitute who was never around. She didn't know who my father was, so I never had the opportunity of meeting him. The only men I met were the numerous johns she brought home to have sex with me. It's strange how there are a lot of men who would rather have sex with a little girl than an adult woman. She would get paid top dollar to watch me have sex with these men. Eventually, I got used to it, but I never forgot.

My mother died when I was seventeen from a drug overdose. I was sad, but I wasn't surprised. I knew that the day was going to come, and I had prepared myself for the day that I would be forced to take care of myself.

I made the transformation from a teenager to a woman quickly and followed in my mother's footsteps, walking the ho stroll and dancing in the strip clubs until I met Earl. Though Earl had ulterior motives for hooking up with me, I believed that he couldn't hide his feelings for me forever. I knew he was married from the start, but I didn't care. I needed that companionship and I sucked up all of the attention he gave me. His promises never fell on deaf ears, and I was so gullible that I believed every word.

Now, after years of working, I was still just a working girl, and Dee was still in charge. I wasn't going to allow this to go on much longer. I was going to get my spot as the HBIC, no matter what it took.

I headed up to my apartment to take a hot bath and drink some tea to soothe my aching throat. I decided to give Earl a call and ask if he could meet with me privately for a conversation. I was nervous about calling because I didn't know if he was still angry with me. He answered groggily as if I had awakened him. I hesitated for a second before speaking.

"Earl, this is Ki-Ki," I said, slowly revealing my identity.

Ki-Ki was the nickname that he gave me a few months after meeting me. I hoped that using it rather that my full name would soften him up a bit.

"What's up? You're calling me at this time of night, so it better be important," he replied with the same tone he answered the phone with.

"We need to talk. I have some information that I think you should know."

"Regarding what?"

"Dee. She's trying to get me out of here for a reason, and I think I've figured it out. I just want to open your eyes to her game before I'm long gone and it's too late."

"So what is this with the two of you? I don't know who to believe. For whatever reason you are both trying hard to get rid of one another, and it's going to end up getting both of you kicked out."

"Earl, all I am asking is for you to hear me out. I'm not trying to play any games with you. Regardless of how you feel about me right now, I still care about you and would hate to see you lose what you've worked so hard to get."

"Lose? What the hell are you talking about Ki-Ki?" he yelled.

"Just come meet with me tomorrow night. I promise this isn't a game."

"You better not be bullshitting me to save your own ass from getting thrown out. I'm a busy man and I don't have time for any games. I'll be there tomorrow at seven PM," he said before quickly ending the call.

Now that I had my meeting with Earl I had the rest of the night to lay out my plan. Dee was so cocky that she would never believe I was smart enough to beat her at her own game. She would definitely think her mind was *playing tricks* on her when I was done with her.

Earl:

Woman Trouble

"Earl, who was that on the phone?" Tina asked after I had ended the call.

I had tried not to wake her, but she had ears like radar when something was going wrong. I turned over, facing her direction, trying to forget the phone call that I had just had. I was anxious to know what it was that Kimona had to tell me. I had an inside source that I thought was being totally honest with me, but obviously that wasn't a fact.

"That was just one of my employees, babe."

I knew she thought I was lying. I had cheated on her so much in the past that she couldn't think of me doing anything else but that.

I mean, I love my wife, but I am sometimes led astray. Kimona was definitely much more that just an employee; she was once a major part of my life. When I met her I knew that there was something different about her. Her looks definitely made her stand out, but I could tell that she had been through something growing up. I wanted to be there for her, and I had been for a long time.

Other than my wife, she was the only woman that I could see myself growing with. As a married man, I shouldn't have had those thoughts, but I couldn't get her out of my mind. I was more hurt than angry when Dee told me that she'd been stealing from me. I would do anything for her, and as much money as she made, there was no reason for her to steal. I had to find out what was really going on at Allure, and I was sure that one of these women wasn't telling me the truth.

Looking at my wife made it easier for me to clear my plans for tomorrow out of my head. Even after having our children she was as perfect as the day I met her. Nothing was out of place; not even a stretch mark was left behind as proof of childbirth. She had her eyes closed, but the faint blinking let me know that she was still awake.

I leaned in and kissed her, instantly focusing on making love to her. Her body was warm and soft as I rubbed my hand across her back. Her eyes were now open and looking back at me.

She smiled as she felt my member finding its way through my boxers. Still lying face to face, she grabbed hold of my throbbing pole and massaged the head of it with the pre-cum as lubrication.

I let out a sigh as I tried to hold back an early eruption.

Soon her head disappeared from in front of me and was beneath the plush comforter. I felt her lips wrapping around it while I watched the blanket move to the rhythm made with her head. Her mouth was soaking wet and I slowly moved back and forth, guiding myself in and out of it. I could hear the muffled sounds of her sucking, which turned me on even more than I had been a few minutes earlier just looking at her.

I could feel my heart pounding, and I knew that I couldn't take any more of her French kissing or I'd be exploding. I grabbed hold of her, signaling her to stop. She eased up from under the covers and we were now face to face again. I nudged her on the shoulder so she could turn around with her back facing me. Our chemistry was so tight, most times we didn't have to say a word to know what the other one was thinking. She leaned forward just enough to push her ass close to me.

Raising one leg up, I easily entered her from behind. The juices inside of her instantly began to flow, wetting my member from end to end. Her walls felt like a hand with a tight grip, and again I tried hard not to end this episode too early.

As I moved forward she moved backward; our bodies in sync had me feeling like a kid in a candy store. I could feel the sweat forming on her back as I placed one hand there to give myself more leverage.

I picked up speed as she reached back and grabbed hold of her ass cheek to open up a little more. I slid right in deeper, and she moaned in satisfaction. I responded with a sigh and followed that with slow circles. I had one leg up in the air like a dog trying to get as deep as I could. I reached around and grabbed one of her breasts and began kneading it like dough. Her nipple was hard and slipping through my fingers as I got too excited to hold on tight.

By now Tina was nearing her orgasm. I could tell by the way she was clawing at the bed and gnawing at the sheets. Even at my age I still had it. I was proud that I could still make my wife cum after seventeen years of marriage. Not too many couples even have sex after ten years, but we had managed to keep the fire going.

"Are you cumming, baby? I need you to tell me when you're cumming." I was breathing heavily, trying to hold on to my orgasm until she was able to reach hers.

"Oh shit, baby . . . I'm cumming!" She screamed so loud, I thought for sure she would wake the kids.

It didn't take more than a few seconds to follow in her footsteps to orgasmic ecstasy. My love poured inside of her and began to seep out the sides. We lay still for a few seconds until my now limp member eased its way out of her love nest and onto my thigh. I was exhausted, but the workout was well worth it.

I watched my wife get up to head to the bathroom. One thing about Tina, she refused to let another woman take away what she had worked so hard to maintain. If she thought that I was itching to head out and screw someone else, she'd put it on me ten times better than normal so I wouldn't want to screw anyone or I'd be too tired to do it. She had better game than any NBA player, and though I was on to it, I believed that any woman willing to deal with all of the shit I'd put her through deserved the best.

I hadn't hesitated giving her the best either. From cars to clothes to jewels, she had it all. She left the house each day looking like she was in a beauty pageant. I couldn't complain, though, because she kept it tight for me.

After she disappeared into the bathroom I began thinking about the brief conversation I had with Kimona. As hard as I tried not to let it, it kept coming back. Even after the knockout sex I'd just had, I still couldn't clear my head.

I had to give Brandy a call to see if there was anything new going on in the house. She had been my eyes and ears for the past few months. I can admit that I had knocked her off a few times, but there weren't any feelings behind it, just sex. I wondered what the hell Kimona could possibly have to tell me that Brandy hadn't already told me.

See, Brandy was one that I would have never expected to be a snitch, but I guess everyone wanted their chance to be at the top. The first time I had sex with her was when she approached me one evening after I had left the building and asked if we could take a ride to talk. I wasn't sure what we needed to talk about, but when she mentioned that it involved my money, I quickly agreed to the ride.

I told my driver to take a ride around the park while we sat in the backseat and talked.

"So, what's been going on at the house?" I asked, not really aware of her intentions.

"Dee and Kimona both are playing you. I've sat back and watched the two of them fight like cats to get the top spot, but while they are trying to set each other up, you are getting the short end of the stick."

"What do you mean by that?"

"They've both been stealing from you; Dee is definitely calling the kettle black when she blames everything on Kimona. She's lied to you about some of things she's done, to try and get Kimona out of there. She had cameras set up everywhere, and when Kimona was almost killed by that customer it was only because she told him to be rough with her. The reason Kimona had men coming to her apartment was because Dee hasn't been giving her all of her money. I guess she figured she had to get her money somehow."

"So, Dee is the reason Kimona was stealing from me?"

"Now, I'm not saying she's Ms. Innocent, by a long shot. I've been running the books, so I know that she hasn't been turning her slips in. The money from the bar and drugs was coming up short. I know that this is a lot to take in, but I can be your eyes and ears if you need me to be."

By now, her hands were resting on my thigh. I knew where this was leading, but her offer did sound good. I needed someone to watch both of them. They both seemed to be running a scam on me, and I wasn't about to have that happen for too much longer. I told her that I would pay her extra on the side to keep me up on what was going down at Allure and she agreed.

Soon her hand moved from my thigh to massaging my dick through my slacks. I could feel her breath on my neck, causing me to get hard as rock down below.

I grabbed hold of her hand and stopped her for a minute. "What's your angle, Brandy? Are you trying to fuck me so that you can run Allure?"

"No, I'm trying to fuck you because that's what I want to do. I've always wanted a piece of you. I have to see for myself why two beautiful women are going crazy over you," she replied, as her hand began to ease right back into the position of massaging my responsive member.

I decided not to speak another word because I was definitely turned on. The driver even adjusted his mirror, trying to take a peek as what she would do next.

She unzipped my pants to release my hardness and began rubbing it on her face, glazing her lips with my pre-cum. This girl was a freak, and I was anxious to see just how freaky she could get in the small quarters of this backseat.

She licked the head continuously, like she was trying to find out how many licks it took to get to the center. If she kept this up, there would be cream all over her face because I couldn't stand much more. Before I knew it, she was deep-throating me, rubbing my dick on her tonsils. It was at this point I thought about adding her to the lineup because she damn sure had the head game on lock.

My mind was racing as the driver continued to make circles around the park. The air was blowing in from the open sunroof, and I had my head back looking out at the sky, while she continued to make love to me with her mouth.

I lifted up her dress to take a peek at her firm, round ass. She had on a black thong that was placed right in the middle of her juicy pussy. My arms were pretty long, since I stood about 6-3, so they were long enough to reach around and massage her hot nest. She had the fattest pussy I had touched in years. I wondered how a woman that small could have such a fat pussy. That was neither here nor there; I just got sidetracked for a second, but now I was back thinking about waxing her fat ass!

She continued to go up and down my shaft for what seemed like a half inch at a time. I was raising my butt off the seat to get every inch inside of her mouth. She didn't have a problem fitting it in either. I wanted to fuck her and I had to get to it quick before she'd assume I was a minute man.

"Come on and let me feel that wet pussy wrapped around my dick," I said, in a Barry White tone.

"You want to feel this pussy?"

"Damn right, I want to feel it."

"I need you to taste it first so you can see how sweet it is," she replied, leaning her back against the door and putting one leg on the top of the seat and one on the floor, then pulling her panties to the side.

I wasted no time assuming the position in front of her pussy, which was now staring me in the face. I stuck out my tongue and gave it one good lick from top to bottom. She moaned and released her round breasts from her dress. I sucked on her clit slowly and would occasionally let it slip out of my mouth, causing her to shake a little.

Her pussy had the scent of mangoes and the taste of heaven. I stuck one finger inside, then turned my hand around to reach her G-spot. I played with it while still sucking on her clit until her cream was all over my face and she was shaking uncontrollably.

I laughed while sitting up looking at her paralyzed state. She was still biting her lips and holding on to her left breast.

"Come fuck me now," I instructed.

I massaged my dick to keep it standing at attention. We were still driving around the park, and the driver was still enjoying the show.

She climbed on top of me and began riding me like a horse at a rodeo. Her pussy was so warm, I felt like a heating pad had just been wrapped around my dick. She reached her hands outside through the open sunroof and grabbed hold of the roof as a handle, her breasts were bouncing as she leaned back and fucked me in a grinding motion.

She was damn near on the driver's back and still able to maintain the motion. "Is this pussy good to you?" she asked, taking a second to look me in the eye.

It was hard for me to say a word because she was working me like a professional. "Damn good!"

She began screaming, nearing another orgasm, I assumed. She was fucking me faster and faster. I couldn't control myself; I grabbed hold of her breasts and erupted. I could feel cum shooting out of me. I began to shake and scream her name. She had me in the backseat yelling like a little girl. I don't know if it was the excitement of the scenery or if it was just because she was beast. Whatever it was, I had never experienced an orgasm like that, and I definitely planned on coming back for more.

* * *

I snapped back to reality when my wife entered the bedroom. She crawled back in bed and I eased out to go clean myself up and sneak to the phone to call Brandy. Once I was down in the living room I used my cell to call her up. She answered on the second ring.

"Brandy, it's Earl."

"Hey, Earl. What's up? You haven't paid my pussy any mind lately. She's missing you over here in the cat house."

"I know, baby. I'll check you out soon. How are things over there at the house?"

"Same as always. Dee is still up to her shit, and so is Kimona."

"You sure it's the same? I don't want anything sneaking up on me. I'm paying you good money to watch the house for me."

"If anything different happens, I'll make sure I let you know. I wouldn't keep you in the dark like that."

"All right, I have to go. Wifey is still up. Talk to you later."

"OK, good night!"

I hung up the phone and headed back up to bed, now even more anxious about tomorrow's meeting with Kimona. I needed to see which one of them was out to destroy me. I had more "woman trouble" than I could stand right now. I closed my eyes and hoped to at least have a good night's sleep.

Kimona:

Eye on the Prize

"Come on in and have a seat," I said, as I put on the sexiest tone I could muster up.

Earl wasn't amused as he stepped into my apartment and looked around. He appeared to have his guard up, so seducing him at this point was out of the question. I watched him walk around my living room as if he was expecting to find something.

I missed him, and it had been a long time since we'd been in a room together alone. I wanted to jump all over him and tell him that I had done the things I'd done for him, but I knew he would never believe me until I let him see the wool Dee was trying to pull over his eyes.

"So, what is it that you have to tell me about Dee?"

"She hasn't been completely honest with you, and she's been making some money of her own on the side."

"Really? Just like you were doing? I guess I've lost my eye to scope out thieves," he responded sarcastically.

"Earl, I know that Dee mentioned she wanted to have men working in the house, right?"

"How did you know about that?"

"Because I've been watching her just as she was watching me. The only difference is I'm doing it from the heart. I care about you, Earl, and I want to you know who's here to hurt you."

"So what's the point?"

"She's not only been interviewing men, sexing them in her office and including Brandy in on all the sessions, but she's been having them work and not telling you. Instead she's been keeping the money all to herself."

"What?"

"Yes, she has them working already, even though you haven't approved it."

"So you're telling me she blatantly ignored what I said and has been collecting money without telling me?"

"That's what I'm telling you." I moved a little closer to the spot where he'd been standing.

He sat down on the sofa and placed his hands over his face. "I can't believe this shit. After all the shit that I've done for her, she goes behind my back like this."

"I'm sorry I had to be the one to tell you, but I told you from the day you hired her that I should have been in her place. I've been setting her up all along. I knew that she would try to set me up and lose sight of what she was trying to do. She thought she had everything in the bag, but you let me stay and I've made my quota."

"So why should I believe you now? You admitted to stealing from me."

"I know I did, but I kept all of the money and planned on investing it into your company. I just needed time to show you what I planned on doing."

"Investing? Ki-Ki, what the hell are you talking about?"

"I know that you are upset right now, so you probably won't understand where I'm coming from, but I promise to have all the details to you in a few days. I don't want to upset you, trust me. I want to make you feel good," I said, standing in front of him and placing my hand on his shoulder.

I wanted to make love to him. It had been such a long time since he'd touched me, and I was definitely missing out. "Can I make you feel good?" I asked, taking the chance of being rejected.

He didn't respond, only sitting back on the chair and staring at me. He had resisted me for a long time, but he was hurt and confused right now, so he was vulnerable.

I was ready to take full advantage of that. I got on top of him as his back rested against the sofa. We stared at each other without saying a word.

I leaned in to meet his lips, hoping that he would respond. He reached up with one hand and lightly grabbed the back of my head to guide him in the sensual kiss I yearned for. I instantly became wet from the anticipation of him touching me.

I had on a robe but was naked underneath because I knew that this was sure to turn him on. Even when Earl was upset he couldn't resist me.

I opened my nightgown to release my extremely hard nipples from confinement. He began to massage them and lick and suck them, each motion in a flawless rhythm.

I loved the sounds he made while he did this, and I also loved the feeling of his dick growing underneath my pussy. I knew that he could feel the heat. I was on fire and was using every morsel of energy I had to contain myself.

"I miss tasting these; it's been a while," he moaned.

I started to grind on his hard dick through his pants. My pussy juices were rubbing all over his pants. I was close to cumming just because I was so excited, and the friction of rubbing against was intensifying the feeling. I couldn't waste time with foreplay. I wanted him deep inside of me immediately.

I loosened his belt and unzipped his pants, releasing his manhood. I grabbed a condom from my end table and opened it. I slid it on after rubbing the pre-cum off and sucking it off of my finger. The taste was sweet, getting me more excited as it eased down my throat.

I turned around so that my back was facing him, bent over, and sat on his dick. I wiggled until I got it all the way in then I sat there on it for a few seconds, to feel it throbbing inside of me.

I rose up and slammed my ass back down, pausing for a second each time. Next I would do a circling motion to tap my G-spot a few times before lifting back up. I would rise up just enough so that the head stayed inside and then with force push it all back inside.

He loved it, and he was holding on to my waist tighter than GI Joe with the Kung Fu grip. My fat ass was bouncing and making a loud smacking sound when I touched down.

He couldn't take it; he pushed me off of him and stood up, dropping his pants down to the floor. He removed the condom and stood still in front of the sofa, jacking off slowly. "Come suck this dick," he instructed.

I got in a squatting position in front of him and grabbed hold of it. His dick was one of the most perfect sights I had seen. I kissed the head as if I was kissing his lips.

"Just like that, you know how Daddy likes it," he moaned.

I continued to suck his dick like it was a Blow Pop and I was trying to get to the bubble gum inside. My jaws were tight, and my mouth was full and juicy. His hands were on the back of my head, and my free hand was down below, fingering my pussy. I needed his dick back inside of me.

Once he'd had enough sucking, he told me to lie on the coffee table and open wide. I did as I was told and played with my clit until he came closer. With his legs on both sides of the table he got down low and reintroduced his dick to my pussy, which was more that happy to meet him.

His rhythm was sending me wild; I couldn't hold it in any longer. Within a few seconds I could feel the rush of my juices pouring out like a faucet.

"I can feel you cumming, baby. Damn, this shit is wet. I'm getting ready to cum too, I need to cum in your mouth baby. Would you like that?"

"I would love it baby . . . . Shit, I'm cumming again," I yelled as my body began to tremble all over. Back-to-back orgasms were something amazing.

He gave a few more pumps before he pulled out, walked up, and bent down so I could suck the cum out of his pulsating dick. I raised my head just enough, took him in my mouth, and sucked him dry, not releasing one drop. He was standing there holding on to his dick, shaking like he was having a seizure. I was smiling inside because I knew that I had done a good job.

"You are too much, girl," he laughed, as he picked his pants up from the floor and headed to the bathroom.

After he was done, he told me he would get with me in a few days so I could show him what I had planned as far as investments. I was ecstatic; now I had the chance to really prove myself to him.

After Earl left I felt relieved, because he believed what I told him. At least he appeared to believe me; either way I got my point across. Now, I had to figure out how I was going to present my plan to him in a few days. I wanted him to believe that I was capable of running the show, but I also needed him to trust me. Getting him to trust me was going to be the biggest hurdle for me to jump over.

Honestly, I had taken the money because that bitch Dee was shorting. She thought I didn't know about it, but her slimy-ass assistant Brandy told me everything. She told me how she put a bunch of my tip money in her own stash, and I had a serious problem with that. I knew I couldn't take it back to the streets and whoop her ass, so I had to do it the sneaky way.

The funniest part of it all was that she believed Brandy was on her side. I knew women too well from the streets, and Brandy was definitely one of the most conniving chicks I had ever come in contact with. She was tired of being Dee's slave. Shit, Brandy did most of the work while Dee reaped the benefits of it. On top of that she treated her like she was dog poop on the bottom of her Jimmy Choo shoes.

I knew it would only be a matter of time before she turned on her, and I was right. Brandy confided in me, told me all about the way Dee was trying to set me up. She also told me about the cameras she had posted all over the buildings. Now that I thought of it, I'm sure she'd be pretty pissed when she saw Earl visiting me on the tape.

But back to Brandy, I didn't trust her as far as I could throw her. Behind the scenes I acted as if I liked her and she did the same. I knew that she was good at faking by the way she fooled Dee. She couldn't fool me; I was way too smart for that shit.

I didn't know what her intentions were; however, I did know that she wanted out of the assistant role. So, did that mean we were all aiming for the top? I didn't care how many people I had to compete with to get what I wanted out of this. ***My eye was on the prize,*** and I was going to obtain it regardless of how many scandalous women I had to knock out of my path.

I stayed in my apartment the following day. I didn't even head out to do a lineup. I had some planning I needed to do. My phone was ringing off the hook, and I figured that it was probably Dee trying to find out where the hell I was. I didn't owe her an explanation, and I wasn't in the mood to deal with her arrogant ass today anyway. And as if ringing my phone for hours wasn't enough, someone was knocking at my door.

I walked to the door, annoyed and ready for a fight. I knew that if it was Dee standing on the opposite side when I opened I would be tempted to knock her ass down. Instead when I opened it, I found Brandy standing there with a tape in her hand. *What the hell does she want? And what the hell is on that tape?*

"Hey, Kimona. Can I come in?"

"Sure, why not? What can I do for you?" I said, motioning her to come inside.

"I just wanted to let you know that Dee is pissed that you didn't come to the lineup today."

"Well, honestly, I don't give a damn about Dee or her funky-ass attitude."

"I'm sure, but I wanted to let you know that I noticed that Earl came and spent some time with you yesterday. Luckily I was able to get the tape before Dee got a chance to see it. She would flip if she saw him up in your apartment for over an hour."

"So, are you looking for a thank you? I'm not sure what it is you expect me to say."

"Well, I do expect a thank you. I'm trying to save you

from getting put out of here. Dee is trying any and everything to make sure that you are gone as soon as possible."

"Let me tell you one thing about me, sweetie. There isn't anything that Dee can do at this point to get me out of here. I've made damn sure of that. And me staying in the house isn't something that you should really be concerned about it. You know Dee is shiesty, and I wouldn't be surprised if she was trying to get you put out of here as well."

"I'm not worried about that because I've done a few things to make sure that I won't be going anywhere either. So, do what you want with the tape. You enjoy the rest of your day," she said, before setting the tape on my coffee table and heading toward the door.

I had to think fast. I couldn't let her leave thinking that I hated her. I was still trying to give her the illusion that we were cool.

"Brandy, wait," I blurted out as she grabbed hold of the door knob.

She turned around with an I-told-you-so look on her face.

"Look, I've had a very long day and I didn't mean to be rude. Thanks for the tape, OK?"

"No problem." She smiled, before opening the door and leaving.

It killed me to be nice because I knew that underneath that smile lay a demon. I wasn't about to be tricked. I had been tricked enough to last me a lifetime. I decided to watch the tape to see exactly what was on it. Once I put it in the VCR I sat back on the sofa. Surprisingly, this wasn't a tape of the hall leading to my room. The camera on the tape was pointed right at Dee's desk in her office.

"This dumb bitch gave me the wrong tape!"

Earl:

Crabs in a barrel

After leaving Kimona's apartment I knew that I had to give Brandy a call. I didn't know what the hell I was supposed to believe at this point. It appeared each of them was out to get the other. I was pissed that I had to be put in the middle. I had worked long and hard to get my business to where it was. It definitely didn't come easy, so losing it was out of the question. If I didn't find out the truth about what was really going down at Allure, all of their asses would be hitting the curb.

Before leaving the building I rethought calling her. I was already in the building, so I might as well talk to her face to face. I headed to her apartment and knocked.

She came to the door a few minutes later and seemed startled when she noticed that it was me behind the door. "Earl, what are you doing here?"

"Expecting someone else?" I asked, noticing her lingerie attire.

"No, I'm just surprised to see you, that's all. Come in,"

she said, before moving over to give me space to walk through. "So what brings you here?"

"I came to see how things were going with you. I haven't seen you in a while," I lied, because at this point I could care less how she was doing. My goal was to see which one of them was lying to me.

"I'm doing well. Actually, I was getting a little overwhelmed at one point, but things are going great now."

"What's been going on with my business? You haven't called to give me any updates lately."

"Nothing different, same old stuff, so I didn't want to bother you with it. I honestly didn't have anything to report."

"Really?" I gave her an evil stare.

"Really, Earl. I wouldn't lie to you. Dee and Kimona have been at each other's throats as they normally are."

"So what about these men I hear she's been having working here behind my back?"

"Men? Who told you that?"

"It doesn't matter who told me, what matters is if it's true or not. I can't have anybody stealing from me."

"There aren't any men working here, I can promise you that. If anything like that was going on, I would know about it."

"I've heard different, Brandy, and quite frankly, I'm tired of the bullshit. I can't seem to get the truth out of anyone around here," I raised my voice. I was determined to get my point across.

"Earl, I am telling you the truth."

"I have some other business to take care of, but I'm going to check in with you in a day or so for an update."

"OK," she replied, before heading toward the door.

Just as I stood up there was a knock at the door. She

turned to look as me as if she was surprised. I returned the stare to see what she would do next. I knew that she must have been expecting someone, and I was anxious to see exactly who it was.

She took a few seconds to open the door and sure enough, there was a man standing there. He stood there staring at me as I did the same.

I decided to introduce myself. "Hey, how are you? I'm Earl, and you are?" I extended my hand.

"The name is Supreme. Nice to meet you, Earl."

"OK, Supreme, you two have a good time though. I'm sure you already know how she gets down." I laughed a little.

"What is that supposed to mean?" he replied, seemingly annoyed by my comment.

"Nothing, man. Just have a good time." I laughed again.

I was in no mood for a fight, but I would have his black ass thrown out of there in a second. I had other things to handle, so I didn't have time to continue the conversation.

As I headed out I thought more about him, though. Supreme sounded like some sort of stage name. I wondered if this was one of the men Dee had working there. If so, what the hell was he doing in Brandy's apartment?

My next stop was to Dee's office. I wanted to see if she would incriminate herself any more, since all three of them seemed to be doing it so easily.

Dee was sitting at her desk when I entered the office without knocking. She seemed startled, which was the effect I was going for. I didn't want her to see that I was coming. I soon found out that she didn't have enough time to shut off her TV before I came in. The view was just what I needed to see.

"So what it this? Why all the cameras?"

"I need to keep an eye on everything that's going on around here. That's how I make sure your money is right."

"So is my money right?"

"Of course, now that Kimona is under control, everything is running smoothly"

"Under control, you really believe that?"

"Yes. Should I have a reason not to?"

"So who's Supreme?"

"Supreme?"

"Yes, the guy that you're watching Brandy fucking on TV. Who is he?"

"I don't know who he is; I guess he's one of her friends."

"You guess? I thought you knew everything that was going on around here? I guess that wasn't a true statement, huh?"

I had her right where I wanted her. She was standing there looking like a deer in headlights. She didn't know what to say, and there probably wasn't a lie that she could tell me to clean up this mess.

"I mean, I know he's one of her friends. I just don't know him personally."

"So when are you going to start being honest with me? I've been hearing a lot of things, and none of it is matching what you're telling me."

"I'm not sure what you're talking about, Earl."

"When did I agree to have men working at Allure?"

"You didn't agree to it."

"Well, why am I being told that they are working? Do I look like a fool to you?" I yelled.

I was really getting tired of the games. I just wanted someone to tell me the truth for once. At this point it didn't seem like I was going to accomplish that. I believed Kimona because neither Brandy nor Dee could get their stories straight. She was the only one who had a story consistent with what appeared to be happening.

"No, you don't look like a fool. But do I really look like a liar? Why would I turn on you now? We've built this thing together."

"Together? You haven't helped me build shit! All you've done is run the place for me. You're an employee just like the rest of them. Don't forget where you came from."

"I haven't forgotten, but I work very hard to make sure things work out for you."

"So be honest with me for once. Do you have men working in here?" I gave her another chance. I wanted to see if she really meant what she said.

"No, I do not have men working here."

I gave up. She wasn't going to break, but I knew that I would find out one way or another, and when I did she'd be right back out on the ho stroll. I stared at her silently for a few more minutes before I stood up. I knew she was relieved, but I had something else up my sleeve.

"Give me the tapes." I demanded.

"The tapes? For what?"

"Because the tapes won't lie. I need to see for myself what's been going on around here."

"Earl, there isn't anything on the tape but some of the girls and their clients."

"I don't care, I want to see them."

"But Earl—"

"Give me the tapes, or I will throw you out and look for them myself. Or, better yet, I'll have Brandy come find them for me."

"Brandy? Oh, so she's your source?"

"I didn't say that, and it doesn't matter who my source is. You need to give me the tapes right now."

Eventually, she stopped begging and gave me five tapes. I wasn't sure what I would find on them, but whatever it was had her scared. She tried every excuse in the book to keep me from looking at them. That made it even more important for me to get my hands on them. I left the office without saying another word to her. She sat there looking like a puppy that had lost its favorite toy.

I had control now and couldn't leave the building fast enough to head home and watch the tapes. I left without addressing anyone else. I wanted to keep my presence a little bit discreet. Not everyone needed to know that I was there. I headed home and made it there before my wife. I sat down on the sofa and began watching the tapes.

The first few tapes didn't show much, just some hallways in the building and a few scenes with some of the girls and their clients. I was pretty close to turning it off, until things got interesting. There was my wife in Dee's office. What the hell was she doing there? I was pissed that I couldn't hear what they were talking about. They sat in deep conversation for at least fifteen minutes. I was more confused now than I had been in the last few weeks. I didn't know what reason my wife would have to be down at Allure. Anytime I even asked her to go check up on things for me she said she didn't feel comfortable with that. Now there she was, resting comfortably in Dee's office.

I continued to watch the tape, looking at the clock to see what time it was. I couldn't wait until she strolled in here. I dared her to lie when I had the shit on tape.

After more conversation Dee put a stack of money on the desk, which my wife retrieved and put in her purse. I didn't know what to think. I felt like everyone was trying to shut me down. I couldn't think of anything else. I sat there, anxious and annoyed, waiting for her arrival.

She came home about an hour later. I was still sitting on the sofa with the lights off. I puffed a cigarette and slowly blew out smoke before speaking.

"Hey, babe, why are you sitting in the dark?" she asked, bending down to give me a kiss.

I turned my face to avoid the contact. I was pissed and I wanted her to know it.

"What's wrong with you?"

"What the hell have you been doing down at Allure talking to Dee?"

"She called and said there had been some issues down there and she wanted help straightening it out."

"You said that you felt uncomfortable going down there anytime I asked. Why is that she can make a phone call and you run right down? I'm your husband!" I yelled.

"Earl, it isn't that serious. I was trying to help you out."

"Well, how come you didn't give me some of that money she gave you?"

"What money?" she asked, obviously not realizing that I had it on tape.

"Tina, I saw the shit on tape. I'm tired of everyone lying to me. What the fuck is going on?"

"Don't raise your voice at me, Earl, especially when you don't know what the hell you're talking about."

"I clearly saw you taking a stack of money from Dee and putting it in your purse. What the fuck was the money for? Are you working there or some shit?"

"You can't be serious. Working there? So, you think I'm a ho now?"

"I don't know what to think."

"I told you that she needed some help. She gave me money to hire a private investigator to—"

"You know what, Tina? Forget it. I'm going to stay at a hotel. I can't even stand to look at you right now."

"Earl!" she yelled as I continued to walk away.

I didn't want to leave, and the more I thought about it, the more I changed my mind. I thought of a way to get in her head. I headed back downstairs to where she was sitting on the sofa. She looked up at me, probably thinking I would have my hands full of bags.

"Meet me in the hot tub in ten minutes," I instructed.

"What?" She looked confused.

"I said, meet me in the hot tub in ten minutes and leave the clothes upstairs." I headed down to the hot tub and stripped off all of my clothes before heading in. I was planning on fucking her real good to release some of this anger.

When she walked out naked, I was horny as hell but it was like I didn't see my wife; all I saw was pussy. That probably sounds really messed up, but it was the truth.

As we sat on opposite sides of the hot tub, both of us horny, I could feel my temperature rising far above the hot water. Her round breasts sat just about the water, and I licked my lips as I anticipated the taste of them. The steam was rising, and I slowly moved my hands down to my throbbing dick. She watched as I pleasured myself with my eyes on her.

"Do you want me to taste you?" I asked, as she seemed anxious to be touched.

She nodded her head yes, and I moved close to her. Her hard nipples rubbed against my chest as our lips met, and we instantly began to massage each other's tongues. The sweet taste of her lip gloss excited me as I moved my hands down to her wet pussy. She moaned as I slowly slid one finger at a time deep inside of her. The warmness of her tunnel sent me wild as I moved my kisses from her lips to her neck. She tilted her neck to the side to give me full access.

As the scent of her perfume tickled my nose, I continued to tickle her clit. I instructed her to bend over so that her ass was facing me. With her erect nipples touching the water and her ass in the air, I caressed it while the excess water dripped from her body. Tina's perfectly round ass was just waiting to be kissed, and soon I was planting French-inspired kisses all over it. I stiffened my tongue and began to massage her asshole, which was delivering sweet nectar to my taste buds. I held on to her waist to force my tongue deep inside until she couldn't take anymore.

Next she sat on the edge of the hot tub with her legs opened wide. Her juicy mound was like art and deserved delicate attention. I got on my knees and stared at her wetness as she held the lips open for me. I slowly licked her clit, making figure eights with my thick tongue, and it was sending her wild. I sucked on her wet clit and slowly let it slip from my lips a few times before burying my face deep inside.

I was fucking her with my tongue, and she was palming the back of my head for a deeper grind. She began to tremble as she reached her peak. I kept going to initiate more, and I sucked up all the cum she released.

She sat on the edge of the hot tub, exhausted and waiting to return the pleasure. I was ready as I stood up over top of her. With one leg over her shoulder she began to suck on my rock-hard dick. I rocked my hips back and forth, fucking her face.

"Right there!" I spoke as I enjoyed letting my pre-cum run down her chin.

She wrapped her hands around my shaft as I began to move up and down like I was deep inside of her pussy.

"Keep jacking me off, just like that!" I yelled as I stood over top of her, nearing an orgasm.

It wasn't long before I was cumming all over her face and barely able to stand. I sat down next to her as she licked her lips. This experience was something much different. I couldn't even come up with a word to describe how I felt afterwards.

I couldn't wrap my mind around what was going on. I tried to think back to figure out how things got so crazy, and I still couldn't figure it out. What is a man supposed to do when he can't even trust his wife? Was money that important to cause these women to get so vicious? They were like female ***crabs in a barrel,*** pulling the other back in each time they got to the top. I refused to be pulled down with them. I was going to come out of this on top, just as I'd always done when a curve ball was thrown my way.

Kimona:

The Tape

I couldn't erase the big smile off of my face. I didn't even have to work to get the goods on Dee. And, Brandy, how stupid could you be not to watch the tape before giving it to me? This was all I needed to bury Dee's ass. Soon, I would be running Allure, and her black ass would be right back out on the strip. As many times as she'd tried to get me out of there for stealing, she was doing the same thing.

There Dee was, sitting at her desk, doing an interview. I couldn't hear anything on the tape, so I assumed that her camera didn't have any sound. I knew that it was an interview by the way the man was dressed. I could see his profile, but not his full face because he was turned to the side.

They talked for a few minutes before he stood up from the chair and began to remove his clothing. He dropped each piece on the floor and never lost eye contact with Dee, who was still sitting in her seat. He mumbled something to her, and she smiled before rising up out her seat.

He was still standing in the same spot, but now only wearing his boxers. I could tell by the bulge in front that he was working with something. Shit, I kind of wished it was me on that tape getting a taste of the dark-skinned stranger.

She came over and rubbed her hands across his sculpted chest. She motioned with her hand, and soon Brandy appeared on the tape. She took Dee's position in front of him and rubbed on his manhood through his boxers while sucking on his nipples. Dee was now taking off her clothes and enjoying the view. I was getting excited just watching, and I tried to contain myself, as it continued to turn me on.

From behind, Dee slid off his boxers and his rock-hard dick was staring Brandy in the face. She grabbed it and slowly licked the head before deep-throating every inch of it. As good as she was giving him head, she needed to be one of the workers rather than Dee's assistant. Her head was bobbing back and forth as Dee was in back of him whispering in his ear. He seemed to be enjoying himself as both of them continued to work on him.

Dee came around and began to undress Brandy and she continued to give head to the man whose face I still didn't recognize. Dee got down on the ground and slid under Brandy, beginning to give her pussy sweet kisses. I was getting hotter as I began to squirm in my seat. Brandy was in a squatting position, grinding into Dee's face while she massaged his balls and sucked on his pole like an ice-cold Popsicle. Her breasts were bouncing up and down, and she began to get excited and fuck Dee's face faster. Dee was finger-fucking herself while taking all of Brandy's juices in.

The stranger soon took control and motioned for Brandy to get up. He instructed Dee to lie on top of the desk. She obeyed and spread her legs wide open. He bent Brandy over the desk so she could return the favor to Dee while he fucked her from behind. Her firm ass was up in the air as he pulled her cheeks apart to take a peek. He shook his head in approval, I assume, as he used his hands a guide to stick his dick inside of her. He slowly stuck in his dick, keeping her cheeks spread apart.

At the same time, she was sucking on Dee's clit while Dee grabbed the back of her head and grinded into her face, lifting her ass off of the desk to get a deeper grind. Dee was fucking her face like it was a stiff dick. The stranger was still fucking Brandy from behind, holding on to her hips like handlebars.

I could see Dee begin to shake as she came. Brandy didn't change her position, only eating her pussy a little harder. She was getting fucked from behind with so much force. Dee had a bunch of her hair in her hands and still fucked her face.

I was getting hornier by the second and was now playing with my clit. My pussy was dripping wet and needing to be fucked. I stuck two fingers inside of my throbbing pussy, still watching them devour Brandy. She was enjoying the pleasure they were giving, while I was enjoying watching it.

The stranger had one leg up like a dog, with his arms on her waist, fucking her harder and harder. My fingers were going in and out my pussy like they had a mind of their own. I was moaning and rubbing my breast through my bra.

On screen, Dee and Brandy had now switched places. Brandy was up on the desk doggy style, and Dee was eating her ass. Brandy was throwing her ass back, like she had been on the dick a few minutes before. They were all in unison, all in a row satisfying each other.

I couldn't stop moaning. You would have thought I was getting that dick inside of me the way I was going crazy. The scene excited me so much, I felt like I was right there in the room with them.

He was bending down, pushing up and doing all kinds of trick moves behind her ass. I knew that she must've hired him because he was definitely a doggy-style champion. Brandy was finger-fucking herself as I had been doing, while Dee continued to eat her from behind.

I was getting close to an orgasm. I removed my fingers from my pussy and began rubbing them against my clit to get closer to that good ol' feeling of bliss. I was moaning louder and louder.

By now the stranger had removed his dick from Dee and was jacking off right over top of both of their faces. They were down on their knees with their eyes closed and their tongues out waiting to taste his lava.

Just as he exploded and they both had cum all over their faces, I had cum all over my fingers. I was satisfied and I knew that I would have to make a copy of this tape to keep around. I had never been so excited by a tape; I guess I never knew how seeing someone I knew fucking would affect me. I knew now.

After watching the tape, I felt relieved. Now I just had to wait to hear from Earl, to show him what I had found. Our meeting was set for the following day, and I was well prepared for it.

When he arrived, I smiled. He had the same bland expression that he always had on his face, except for when he was getting some head or something. It didn't bother me one bit because I knew he would be proud of what I had brought to his attention. He came in and sat down, not saying a word. I was going to wait around to see what he had to say, but I decided to just start off the conversation since he seemed to be in a bad mood.

"So, I have this tape of Dee and Brandy screwing all of the men she hired."

"Another tape?"

"Another one? What do you mean?" I asked puzzled.

"I've seen enough shit to last me a lifetime, but if you tell me that it is something on this tape worth watching, then so be it."

"OK," I replied before heading to the TV to play the video for him.

He sat there watching the first few minutes of each scene before fast-forwarding it. I figured he was in no mood for porn. It was incriminating both of them, and there wasn't anything they could say to explain why they had been interviewing and sleeping with these men.

He continued the same order until the tape was through. He sat there still silent after the tape stopped. I didn't know what to say because I wasn't sure if showing him the tapes helped me or not.

"You know, you are about the only one that I trust. I never thought I would be saying that to anyone but my wife, but I don't know who to believe. I've seen a lot and heard a lot the past few days, and I just have to get my head straight to know where I am headed."

"I know this is a lot for you, Earl, and I hate to see you upset, but I had to show you what they were doing to you. I told you from the beginning that I should have been running Allure, and you thought that I was a better lay than a businesswoman. But look at me now, Earl. I've changed, and I'm capable of running the business."

"I know that you are capable of that, Ki-Ki, and I wish

that I would have listened to you back then. Maybe I wouldn't be in the position that I am now. This shit isn't only ruining my business, but it's doing the same thing to my marriage. I didn't come into this game for this."

"Again, Earl, I'm sorry, and if there is anything that you need me to do for you, I'm here. I am ready to step up and get things in order for you."

"I really appreciate that, and I will be making a lot of changes around here very soon. You can be sure of that."

He stood up and gave me a hug before leaving.

Damn, I don't know what had Earl so messed up. I knew that he would be upset about the tape, but not like this. He was more hurt than angry, and that was a side of Earl that I had never seen before. He said that it was ruining his marriage, which was another thing I didn't understand. Because how Allure would have anything to do with his home life? I guessed that I would soon find out.

I still had some things to work out. I had to figure out how I was going to get the title of madam. Even if I managed to get Dee and Brandy out of there, it didn't guarantee my spot. For now I was relying on ***the tape*** that would show him what they were doing, with the hopes that he would believe that I was out for his best interest and he'd have no choice but to put me in charge. I was praying that this would work because, right now, this was my only option.

Earl:

The Round Table

I called a meeting with Kimona, Dee, and Brandy at Allure. I needed to talk to them all at once to see how they would act. Now that my wife was caught in the mix somehow, I had to end this situation as quickly as possible. I got all the tapes together, including the tape that Kimona had given me, and headed down to the meeting. I didn't tell them that I was meeting them all at once, and I knew that they would be surprised once they all came in and saw each other. My plan at this point was pretty simple: The liars had to go, and the one left standing would be running Allure.

As I sat in the meeting room at the table, I was setting up a presentation like I was presenting to an executive board. I was ready to see their jaws drop, with all of the evidence I had.

Dee was the first to enter the office. She tried to find out what the meeting was about, but I didn't answer her. I sat silent, waiting for the rest of them to arrive.

Kimona was next to enter the room, and once she saw Dee, her smile instantly turned into a frown. "What the hell is she doing here?" Kimona said, one hand on her hip.

I could see a catfight nearing, and though I would love to see which one of those two would win, I didn't have time for that right now. "I need to meet with her as well, so please have a seat," I instructed.

"Well, what are we waiting for?" Dee asked, becoming impatient.

Brandy walked into the room and you could see the anguish on all of their faces. I had succeeded in the jaw-dropping effect I was going for. None of them knew what to expect. Brandy eased down in her chair without saying a word. They all looked at each other then turned to look at me.

I smiled because inside I knew that this situation was about to boil over. I stood up to begin talking, gaining all of their attention immediately. "So, ladies, I called this meeting because things have been getting out of hand here at Allure, and I need to get them back in order. Dee, I hired you to run this place, hoping that I wouldn't have to be around as much. Lately, that's been impossible. I trusted you, and instead you went behind my back and collected funds that I didn't know anything about."

"Earl, we've already discussed this, and why do we have to do this here?"

"You're absolutely right; we did discuss this already, but that was before I had this tape." I bent down to turn the tape on showing Dee interviewing the men and setting them up with customers.

She sat there stunned, probably wondering how I got my hands on this tape, which wasn't one of the tapes that she'd given me.

"Where did you get this tape?" she asked, looking at both Brandy and Kimona.

Neither one of them budged. They were both out to get Dee, so of course, they wouldn't say a word. She got angrier by the second.

"Which one of you bitches ratted me out?" she screamed, but they still sat silent. "I'm not going to sit here and be attacked. I'm out of here," she said before standing.

"Sit down, because I'm not done talking!" I yelled. This childish shit had to stop. Someone was going to take responsibility for her actions today.

"Then, there is my lovely wife who is on video taking money from you. I guess it wasn't very hard to get her in on your madness, huh? You must be a better lover than me or something, because I couldn't even get her to darken the doorstep down here."

"I can explain that, Earl," she offered.

I quickly rejected the explanation.

"No need, she already did it for you. Neither one of you are going to be honest about what the money was really for, but I don't care. It doesn't even matter anymore."

"Yes, it does matter, Earl. I can really explain what the money was for," she pleaded.

Her begging was going in one ear and out of the other. I had already made up my mind what I was going to do. I just wanted to rub the lying in her face. Two types of people I hated were liars and thieves, and she was both of those wrapped up in one.

"Moving on to Brandy, I guess you didn't think that this was about you either? Well, you're wrong if you did. I have tapes here of you joining in the interviewing with Dee. You tried to turn on Dee, making me believe that it was all her, but I clearly see you fucking on this tape as well."

"You little bitch!" Dee yelled, before jumping across the table and wrapping her hands around Brandy's neck. She pulled her onto the table and began hitting her on the top of her head.

I quickly broke them up, but not before Brandy retuned a few of those punches. I sat Dee back down in her chair as she continued to scream obscenities at Brandy. Kimona was still sitting comfortably on the sidelines, watching with a smile on her face.

"Brandy, I trusted you too. I asked you to be my eyes and ears down here. You promised me that you would let me know everything that was going on, but instead you were in on it."

"I can explain—"

"This isn't the time for explanations. I gave you a chance to do that, and you lied. You told me that there weren't any men working at the house. Here it is on the tape, clear as day. You couldn't be honest and let me know what was going down. Now you are ass out!"

"So what does that mean?"

"It means that both you and Dee can carry your black asses up to your apartments, get your shit, and get the hell out of Allure."

"Are you serious, Earl?" Dee asked, confused.

"I'm as serious as a heart attack."

"So what about Kimona? All of the scheming that she's done, she should be leaving too."

"Actually, she's staying, and she'll be taking your spot."

"I worked too hard to be on top, Earl. You can't do this to me."

"You've both done it to yourselves."

Brandy stayed quiet as tears began to form in her eyes. I wasn't sure what she planned to gain by helping Dee, but whatever it was, it landed her on the shit list right along with her. She had potential, and it was a shame that I had to let her go.

When I met Brandy she was a totally different person, but I guess being around Dee so long, her conniving ways rubbed off on her. When she approached me about being the eyes around the house, I was sure that she would most likely end up running Allure. She knew the books—she practically did all the work for Dee—but she was weak. I couldn't have someone who would allow another woman to take over her life the way that Dee had done her. Granted, Dee was her boss, but I'm the one she should have come to from the beginning, instead of lying to me when I confronted her about it.

She sat there continuing to sob as Dee tried to prove her case. I wasn't even listening to her, because as usual, it was a bunch of bull. She had messed up a good thing, and she should have felt sorry for it. Dee wasn't the type of person to give up easily, and the more she tried, the more annoyed I became.

Eventually, she realized that it wasn't working and headed out of the room. Kimona still hadn't said a word, and Brandy still sat there crying.

"Sorry you got sucked in to her madness, Brandy. You could have been on top here."

Brandy looked at me before standing. I assume she figured that there wasn't anything that she could do to change my decision, and there wasn't. I was done with both of them, and though I was pissed, I wished them well. I never wanted to send them back out to the streets that they came from, but they left me no choice.

After Brandy left the room, I looked at Kimona, who was still sitting in her seat. She had never looked more beautiful to me than she did at that moment, and maybe that was because I knew that she had my back. She was the last one standing, and for that, she deserved the top spot.

"Come here," I instructed, motioning with my fingers.

She got up from the chair and made her way over to me. I met her lips with a kiss more sensual than any kiss that I had before. I was excited, and I couldn't wait for the moment when I would quench my newfound thirst with her juices. I wanted to taste her, and she knew it by the way I sucked on her tongue.

I removed her shirt and glanced at her breasts, which were safely nestled in her bra. I lowered her bra straps and sucked on her nipples, getting reacquainted with them both. They were standing at attention, making it easier for me to suck on them, arousing her senses.

She pulled my head up so that I could kiss her again. She slowly pushed me back onto the table and helped me remove my pants and boxers. By now, my pole was standing straight in the air and waiting for some attention. She straddled me and let her breasts dangle over my mouth. I couldn't help to lick them because they were the most perfect set that I'd ever been face to face with. I grabbed them and squeezed them together, trying to kiss both nipples at the same time.

She soon helped me remove my shirt, and while she sucked on my nipples, she used her hands to massage my erect member. She made a path with her tongue all the way down to my belly button and then to the head of my dick, which caused me to let out a sigh. She began feasting on it, licking all around the shaft, taking my balls into her mouth, giving it attention that she'd never shown me before. I guess giving her that position turned her into a beast.

Soon she climbed on top of me and straddled my dick. It was beating like a heart inside of her. Her walls were fitting around it like a glove. I bent my knees and began to meet the thrusts of her pussy as she rode me like the professional that she was. She leaned back and grabbed hold of my knees, using them for leverage. She was riding me like she was a wild bull, and I tried hard to hold my composure. I reached behind her, palming her ass tight, trying to hold my eruption in for a little while longer.

I had to gain control if I wanted to go any further. She was riding me too good, and I was sure to burst any minute with her on top of me. I turned her over so that we could be face to face. I wanted to look her in the eye and see the faces that she made while I hit her G-spot. I used my technique of slow circles with a fast thrust to hit her spot continuously; this was my definition of a nasty grind, and she loved it.

Her eyes were closed, and she bit her bottom lip each time she neared an orgasm. I could feel her juices pouring out each time she came. She was as wet as Niagara Falls and making it easier for me to slide in and out her. She wrapped her legs around my back and held on tight.

I could feel it—I was about to erupt like a volcano, and she wasn't letting go. I moaned, and she joined in. My legs began to tremble, and soon I could feel the fluid rushing out of me. I was drained of all of my energy immediately after that.

I couldn't budge. I lay on top of her for a few minutes while she rubbed my back. I knew she cared about me, and I knew that I had made the right decision putting her in charge.

The round table meeting had started out with me on a path of destruction, and now I was on top of it, floating on cloud nine. What else could a man ask for?

Kimona:

Operation Torri

With both Brandy and Dee out of the way, I now had plenty of time to focus on Torri. She was no longer my competition, and I could use what she had to get what I wanted. I wanted Allure to flourish. Earl wouldn't believe how things could change in a matter of weeks. Everything that I planned worked out for me. I knew that once all of the cards were out on the table, Earl wouldn't have any choice but to let me run Allure. I was more than qualified, and he knew it. Dee tried for a long time to get rid of me, but I wasn't going for it. I had fought all my life for the things I wanted, and I wouldn't stop now. They both underestimated me and ended up with nothing.

I wanted to run things a little differently in the house, and even though Torri was the breadwinner now, she was still going to be included in the lineups. I wanted the customers to have a chance to see all of the women available, including the cream of the crop.

Torri didn't like the idea at first, but after I explained my reasoning, she went right along with it. The way that

I saw things, the more money the better, and any free time is money-making time.

Torri was the kind of female you didn't see coming. She looked so quiet, but she was a stone-cold freak. I couldn't help but wonder how it would be to have a piece of her all to myself. Don't get me wrong; I love dick, but I haven't met a man that could eat pussy as well as a female.

Working at Allure, I had been in many different situations, so it wasn't an issue to be with a woman. If they had the right amount of money, I would work my pussy on them, just like I would on a man making it rain.

I called all of the girls down for the final lineup of the night, but before the lineup I told Torri to sit this one out because I had something special planned for the two of us. She looked at me weird, probably because she didn't know what to expect, especially after what happened with Dee and Brandy.

I needed to get closer to her and make her feel comfortable. I planned on keeping her around for a very long time, and I didn't want her to think that I planned to have her thrown out like them. That was far from my plans; she was a moneymaker, and they were the ones you kept.

The lineup lasted about an hour because we had a lot of undecided customers that night. But after all of that, each girl was picked and heading to private rooms to service the clients.

Torri was sitting at the bar waiting for me after the lineup was done. It had been at least a week since the last time I'd had sex, and I was hornier than a cat in heat. I walked over to her and told her to come over to the lounge and have a seat. She did as I instructed, and I sat down next to her.

"Torri, I just wanted to tell you how good you've been

lately. I don't have anyone here doing as good as you. You remind me of myself when I started out."

"Thanks, Kimona. That is definitely a compliment, coming from you. I know that we started off on the wrong foot, but things have been much better around here lately."

"I'm glad that you feel that way, because I plan to make things a whole lot better for you. I just need you to be my rock around here. You know most of the females here hate my guts, and trust me, they are soon to hate yours too because you are the top chick, just like I was. But you don't have to worry about them. The ball is definitely in your court," I said, placing my hand on her thigh.

She seemed a little uncomfortable at first, probably because we were out in the open. All of the girls were with clients; the only people around were the two bartenders and the waitresses.

I didn't care who saw. Shit, I was running the place now, and I planned on making things work for me. I called one of the waitresses over. She came quickly to see what it was I needed. She bent down so that I could whisper in her ear. I instructed her to bring me a dildo and some whipped cream. Torri continued to look nervous, but soon she would be feeling good.

"Look, you have the opportunity of a lifetime here. I just need you to roll with the punches. I promise I won't steer you wrong. I was your only competition around here, and now you have none. So, you can thank me for that," I said, while rubbing on her thigh.

Her hands were folded across her chest, and she wasn't budging.

My hands soon moved from her thigh to rubbing her fat pussy through her tights. I placed my thumb on her clit that was protruding, since she wasn't wearing any underwear.

She just looked at me, trying to act as if she wasn't amused.

I used my other hand to spread her legs apart and noticed a small slit in her tights, revealing her perfectly shaved landing strip. I continued to rub on her clit and picked up a little speed as she became wetter by the second.

Her hands were now down by her side holding onto the sofa, and her head was lying back on the cushion.

I knew it wouldn't take long to break her.

The waitress soon returned with a silver tray with a huge double-dildo and a can of Reddi-wip. She placed it on the end table and headed back over to the bar, where they were forming to enjoy the show.

I slid one finger in Torri's pussy and continued to play with her clit with my free finger. She was moaning and grinding into my finger.

After a few minutes of letting my finger hit her G-spot, I removed it to add my tongue into the mix. I licked her pussy from top to bottom, side to side, and made circles in the center.

She was now grabbing hold of her breasts and squeezing them for dear life.

Her nectar was glazed all across my face as I dug my tongue in as deep as I could get it. Her legs began shaking uncontrollably as I pumped every ounce of cum out of her.

I took off her shirt and tights and it was then that she was now comfortable with the surroundings. She was feeling good and couldn't care less who was around.

I took the can of Reddi-wip and sprayed it on her nipples and belly button before slowly licking it off of her nipples first. They were hard as a rock, and I could tell she was enjoying it, since her hand was now on the back of my neck. She was getting into it, and that was exactly what I wanted.

After I satisfied both her nipples and my taste buds, I

moved down to her belly button. I sucked all of the remnants of cream out of it and dipped my tongue in a few more times to excite her.

I grabbed the double-headed dildo and rubbed it across her wet pussy a few times before standing up to remove my panties from under my skirt. I stuck the dildo inside of her and began moving it in circles.

She was moaning like crazy.

"You like that shit?"

"Yessssss!" she moaned.

I got on the sofa, my pussy facing hers, and inserted the opposite end of the dildo inside of my throbbing pussy. We both moved to the same rhythm, forcing the still-dick replica inside of each other. I pumped harder while she moved in circles. We were fucking each other like a man would, and it felt amazing. We both raised our hips from the sofa, turning the dildo in circles, hitting our G-spots. Soon we were both shaking and trembling, and cum was running down both ends of the dildo.

The bartenders and waitresses began clapping and blowing whistles. We both picked up our things from the floor and got dressed. Torri looked shocked by their applause. I wasn't affected by it. After all, I loved attention.

"Thanks, Torri. I promise you won't be sorry."

She didn't respond. Instead she headed out of the lounge and over to the elevators. I was glad that I now had her where I wanted her. She was a little nervous, which made my plan for destruction even easier.

I guess she was a little naïve to believe that I wanted to be her friend. It was all a game for me. I wanted to keep her around long enough to make me enough money to really run this place, meaning, me and only me, no Earl or anyone else. Allure would soon be mine, ***operation Torri*** had officially now begun.

Kimona:

Unlikely Source

"I understand exactly what you're saying. I mean, if I were married I wouldn't want my husband running a whorehouse. I would think that he was fucking all of the workers and God knows what else. So, trust me, I feel you," I said.

Tina sat across from me at the desk in my new office. Her relationship with Earl had been in shambles for the past few years, and she thought that getting him out of running Allure would get things back on track. I couldn't say that I wouldn't miss screwing him, but I wanted this place all to myself anyway.

"Anything that you can think of that may potentially get him out of here, I'll go with it. We have a family, children that he never has time for, and me, who rarely even gets hugs and kisses anymore. I miss the man that he used to be. It's really strange to be saying this to someone who has been with my husband, but I have to do what I have to do to save my family."

"I think I know exactly what will work. I may be able to help you out with that, but what will you do for me?"

"I can guarantee that you'll own this building, and I'll give you whatever cash compensation you need. I'm really serious about this."

"OK, I'm thinking this. I have plenty of tapes of Earl and me having sex, so I assume that you don't have a pre-nup right?"

"No, we don't."

"Good. That's even better. You can threaten him with divorce and taking most of what he has. He'll know that a judge will give you what you want when you show them a tape of him committing adultery."

"You really think that will work?"

"I'm positive it will work. We can set up a meeting here. I'll tell him I need to speak with him, and you can be here when he arrives. You will tell him that you have the tapes and that if he doesn't turn Allure over to me you'll divorce him and take everything he has. Earl is all about his money, so I know he will go for it. Plus, I know that he loves you, and once he knows that the reason you were here with Dee was to try the same thing, he'll forgive you for lying. I believe that it will work."

"OK, just tell me the date and I'll be here."

"We can do it as soon as tomorrow if you'd like. The sooner the building is signed over to me, the better."

"No problem. I will see you tomorrow then."

After she left I was relieved. This was going to be much easier than I expected.

I gave Earl a call and asked if he could come down for a meeting the following day and he agreed. I was so excited that I could barely sleep that night. I kept dreaming of what it would be like to be the owner of such a winning establishment.

The following day it was back to business as usual. Torri had been really distant lately, but seemed to be coming around as the days went by. Maybe she thought I would try and seduce her again. That wasn't even in my plans because, the way things were looking now, I wouldn't even need her to win the prize here.

She was still performing great, bringing in the top cash flow in the building. She knew how to work her magic on her customers, and it didn't take long for them to turn into her regulars. She was definitely a hot commodity around here, and as long she didn't cross me, she held her spot here working for me.

I waited all day for the meeting with Earl and Tina. Time couldn't go fast enough. I wanted it so bad, I could taste it.

When the time finally came, I was about ready to burst. When Earl walked in the room and saw Tina sitting in the chair, his jaw dropped like a hot potato. He didn't know what to think.

The two of them made eye contact as I sat there with my elbows resting on the desk, waiting to see which one of them would speak first. My bet was on Earl, and I was right.

"What is this?"

"Earl, sit down. We have to talk," Tina told him.

"Why the hell do we need to talk here, Tina? What is your excuse for being here now? Dee doesn't even work here anymore."

"It's about us."

"What about us?"

"Our marriage. I don't know what happened to us. This place has put a dent in our relationship, and I miss the way things were."

"Why can't we just talk about this at home? This is not the place for this."

"It is the perfect place."

"Why is that? What the hell is so perfect about Allure?"

"I need you to give it up for our family."

"You know I can't do that, Tina. This building has made me a lot of money. It's the reason why we're able to live the way that we do. How can you even ask me to do something like that?"

"Because we can't be happy, as long as it's a part of you. We have to move on."

"And what if I say no?"

"Then I'm going to file for divorce, and I have tapes of you and your mistress here fucking. The judge will pretty much grant me anything I want."

"What? So basically you are threatening me?"

"Earl, I just want the man I married back. Not the man that you turned into once you started running Allure. Things haven't been the same since then. You even make love to me differently, like I'm one of your hoes. We used to make love, Earl. Why can't you see all the pain this is causing me?"

"I see what it's doing, Tina, but it is what pays the bills."

"This is not the only thing that pays the bills. You have plenty of other businesses."

Tears began to drop from her eyes. She was hurting, and you would have to be blind not to see it. I mean, a woman must really love her man if she'd team up with his mistress to get him back. This is something that I wouldn't have believed if it wasn't me sitting there.

"I really have to think about this, Tina. I put my heart and soul into this."

"You put your dick in it too, and that's the problem," she yelled in frustration.

"What am I supposed to do with it? Who am I supposed to sell it to?" he yelled.

"You should give it to Kimona, no sale. Just cut your ties."

"No sale? You are tripping. It's worth too much money to just give away." He began pacing the floor.

"So what am I worth then?" She looked him in the eye with a puppy-dog face that could have won an Oscar.

"You are worth everything, but you have to give me some time to figure this out. I can't just walk away like that. All I'm asking for is a few days to sort everything out."

"A few days, that's all. I really need you to do this for our family."

Earl got down on his knees next to her chair. These two were meant to be together. I had never seen any shit like that in my life. I just wanted him to sign the deed over to me. I didn't feel like seeing a damn soap opera. I would have turned on ABC if I did.

They sat there for a few minutes before leaving. Earl hadn't made any eye contact with me the entire time he was in the room. He was probably uncomfortable sitting in the same place with both of us. The way I saw it, it would only be a matter of time before he gave in. He said that he would in a few days. I had waited this long, so a few more days wouldn't kill me. Now that I had an ***unlikely source*** helping me out, I had nothing to worry about.

Kimona:

Running Smoothly

It had been almost two weeks, and I hadn't heard from either Earl or Tina since the meeting. What the hell was going on? I was becoming more annoyed than anxious now. I wanted to get this over with, so I could move on with my plans. If this didn't work, then I would be forced to go back to Plan A. I hated when things took longer than they should.

I didn't know which way to think. Was she still working on him to get him to give it up? Or had she turned on me? I had been calling her cell phone almost every day, and I hadn't gotten an answer.

I tried to go on with business, but in the back of my mind I kept wondering what they had up their sleeves. Maybe I was overreacting. Maybe there wasn't anything to worry about. As far as I knew, he could walk in there with the paperwork any day, grant me full ownership of Allure. He had no reason not to. He trusted me, or so I believed. We hadn't been seeing much of each other lately, but that was a good thing, because it kept me busy with other things.

Torri was acting strange again, but I tried not to pay

her any attention. Right now she was the least of my concerns. Or should she have been? I didn't know what to worry about. I didn't know which way was up and which way was down. I needed some answers, and just as sure as I begged for one, I got it.

In walked Earl and Tina, all dressed up, looking pretty happy. That instantly put a smile on my face because that meant that I had finally gotten what I wanted. They were going to sign this all over to me. I was practically jumping in my skin. I couldn't let them see how excited I was. I tried to keep my cool as they made their way over to me. I stood there barely able to hold in my smile.

"You want to head to the office and talk?" Earl asked.

"Sure, we can do that."

"And while you at it, call Torri in. I need to say a few things that affect her."

"Torri?" I wondered what the hell she had to do with anything. Then I got this nervous ball in my stomach. Now I really didn't know what they were about to spring on me. I thought that I had it all in the bag, but now things looked a little grim.

I did as he asked, and we all headed to the office. I sat down in my chair as Torri stood by the door. Earl and Tina sat down in front of me.

"So, I've decided to give a percentage of Allure up."

"A percentage?" I asked, confused, because what the hell was I supposed to do with a percentage?

"Yes, I am going to give you fifty percent of Allure."

"Fifty percent, Earl? What am I supposed to do with that?"

"It's more that you have now," Tina interjected.

"I know that, but I don't understand."

"We will be partners, and this is all under one condition."

"What's that?"

"That Torri becomes your assistant."

"What?" I was furious. I'd rather quit than deal with her as an assistant. I didn't need one. I was capable of taking care of things on my own. I had done it so far without anyone. "I don't know why I need an assistant; I have been running everything smoothly since you put me in charge here."

"I know that, but every business owner needs an assistant. You are going to have more responsibility now, and she will be perfect in assisting you."

"But she's our top worker. How can you take her away from that? She brings in more money than three of the other girls combined. We need her to keep the cash flow going."

"I'm sure she'll be just as good an assistant as a worker. You'll find someone just as good as her. You just have to go and recruit someone new."

"I can't agree to that right now, Earl. You should leave things as they are for now. At least, until I can find a replacement for her."

"You know what? That's fair. I'm going to go with that, but you have to get out and begin looking for someone new. I'll give you time to find a replacement, and once you do, Torri will your assistant."

"OK, I will go out and begin looking. Just give me a little time."

He agreed, before they both got up and exited the room.

I was pissed as Torri stood in the corner silently. I knew what I had to do, but now I had to find a way to get rid of Torri because working with her that closely was going to be a problem with me. I didn't really trust her, and I was sure that she didn't trust me.

I relaxed for a few minutes after Torri left the office. I had to clear my head. I was no longer so upset, because I saw a way that it could work. If a new breadwinner was what he wanted, that was exactly what he would get. I had to go out and do some scouting, and I knew exactly where to go.

I headed out to the old strip club where I used to work. There was a girl working there named Cherry I knew would be perfect. Now, Cherry had dancing skills out of this world. I mean, she could climb to the top of that pole and do things with her ass that you wouldn't believe were possible. I knew she was always the last one in the club. Most times she closed and locked it up when her ride was late.

I headed down just before closing time, and sure enough, she was just about the only one left in the club.

"Is that Ms. Cherry I see?" I yelled.

She ran over to me and gave me a hug, "Girl, where the hell have you been? I haven't seen you in so long. You look good, girl," she said, looking me up and down.

"I'm running my own place now."

"Really? So, what brings you to this part of town?"

"I came to see if you would be interested in working for me. I need someone like you on my team."

"How much money is involved? Because you know I make good money here."

"This money ain't shit compared to what you could make with me. This place is exclusive, and only high-paying customers are invited in. With your body and your skills, you would kill them. They'll be asking for you all the time."

"Are you serious?"

"Yes, you can come down and see it for yourself. If you like what you see and you pass the interview, you're in."

"Interview? What is that about?"

"Well, like I said, this place is exclusive, and the customers pay a lot of money for services. You have to be able to please them, and the way the interviews go, if you can please me, you got the job."

"Please you, huh. Now you know my skills firsthand, so I shouldn't even have to do all that."

"That was a long time ago, Cherry, and this is something totally different."

"Well, when do you want to set up the interview?"

"Whenever you want. It's up to you."

"Well, if you wait here until I get out the shower, we can do it right now."

"That's not a problem. I'll just have a seat and wait."

It was about twenty minutes later when she emerged from the back, dressed to kill. I was thinking to myself, *Why get all dressed up to then take clothes right back off?* But I stood up from the chair as she made her way over to me.

I took a deep breath as she put her lips to mine, and I could instantly feel my body temperature rise.

She put her hands on the side of my face to intensify the kiss that sent chills up and down my spine. She was taking control, and it was turning me on.

As her tongue began to massage mine, I used both hands to reach around and unzip her dress. As it fell to the floor, she released her grip and slowly pushed me back to the chair that was seated at one of the small round tables. I sat down and watched as she turned around and bent over to remove her shoes, her ass pointed in my direction.

I reached out to grab it, and she quickly moved away. "Not yet, no touching," she said playfully.

I smiled as I sat back in the chair and continued watching her.

She backed up a little farther and headed to the stereo system. The jazz began to play, and her body began to move to the notes.

It took everything in me not to jump up and tackle her. I wanted to feel her and taste her, but I held it together long enough to enjoy the show.

She slowly unhooked her bra and released one breast at a time. Her perfect nipples stood at attention as she used two fingers to grab hold of them. As she massaged them, she moved her hips in a slow wind. Each time she moved her hips to the front and down to the floor, the lips of her pussy showed from the sides of her thong. She was shaved completely, and I loved it, since I would be able to put the whole thing in my mouth and savor the taste.

She was killing me and she knew it. She turned around and slowly slid her thong over her round ass. Once she stepped out of it, she threw it over her shoulder so I could catch it.

I picked it up off of my lap and put it to my nose. I inhaled the sweet scent of her juices and became even more anxious to taste them.

By this time she was on her knees and bent over on top of one of the tables. She spread her legs and stuck two fingers inside of her tunnel.

I stared as she moved them in and out.

As the juices began to flow, she picked up the pace. She moaned as she reached an orgasm.

I could feel myself getting soaking wet. I stuck my finger into my pants and began to massage my clit. I kept my eyes open, since I didn't want to miss anything. It didn't take long for me to cum as she used her fingers to make love to herself.

She turned around and spread her legs wide. While slowly massaging her clit with one hand, she used her free hand to motion me to come closer. "Come on, taste these juices, I want to fill you up!" she said in a seductive tone.

I wasted no time moving over to the table. I got on my knees and licked my lips, staring at her pussy. I slowly stuck out my tongue and licked her from top to bottom.

She moaned immediately as I began to make circles on her clit. The juices soon began to pour out of her, and I sucked them up, not releasing a drop. I pushed her legs up higher as I stuck my tongue deep into her tunnel.

"Right there, yes!" she said aloud.

Soon she was reaching another orgasm and screaming with delight.

"Come on, baby, let me satisfy you!" she said as I stood up from the ground.

I quickly dropped my pants and stepped out of them. I slid off my underwear.

She instructed me to sit down on the ground. She went to her purse and pulled out what appeared to be lipstick. I wondered what the hell she planned on doing with it, until she removed the top and pressed the button. The tube began to vibrate, and she placed it on my wet clit as I moved my hips to grind against the vibration.

We stared each other in the eye as she used both the vibrator and her fingers to send me wild.

It wasn't long before I had three consecutive orgasms.

She moved up to kiss me, and I closed my eyes, satisfied with what had just happened.

"So did I pass the interview?" she asked, a devilish grin on her face.

She knew damn well she passed, and I couldn't wait to have her working in the house.

I still didn't mention it to Earl because I wanted to hold off as long as I could. I knew he would be checking in with me by the end of the week to see what I had found. I would tell them that no one was quite as good yet until the time was right. Things would be ***running smoothly*** before I knew it. I just had to get a few more things under control, including little Miss Torri.

PART THREE

Torri

BY LAURINDA D. BROWN

Torri:

The Great Escape

I've got to go. I ain't trying to go home, but I got to get the hell out of here.

When I ran away from Cleveland Avenue in Atlanta, the only thing I was concerned about was getting away from my aunt Fatimah and her ignant-ass brother-in-law, Juan, who was supposed to be holding shit down while her husband, Enoch, was doing time for first-degree murder.

Fatimah loved Enoch and was usually the reason he got out of shit when he'd fucked up. One time Enoch and his boy Roc was doing these smash-and-grab robberies out in Buckhead, taking thousands and thousands of dollars in high-end jeans. Enoch was bold as hell, but that nigga Roc was a bit scary. This idiot took the jeans down to The Underground and was selling them for fifty dollars on the corner. Those were three-hundred-dollar jeans! Anyway, this lady kept coming by the table asking a whole bunch of questions, and you could tell from a mile away she was the po-po. Every time she'd leave, Roc would get on the phone and call Enoch.

Finally, he got Fatimah in on the scheme, and let me tell you, the girl was no joke when it came to falsifying documents and creating a paper trail. With a scanner and a little magic from Microsoft Office, she hooked Roc up with some receipts and invoices. Made it look like they came straight from Taiwan.

What got Enoch locked up, though, was the bullet he put in Roc's head for stealing from him.

One day after school, I came in and found Fatimah riding Juan on my bed. They didn't see me, though. I mean, I knew Juan had been hitting it for a good minute. Hell, Fatimah was always walking through the house in nothing but her underwear, so Juan was simply being a man. You see, fucking around with your man's family is some Maury Povich shit, if you ask me.

Enoch had been in jail for about three years, but Fatimah had a two-year-old she had the nerve to name Enoch Jr. He looked just like Enoch, but all them Underwoods looked alike. Most of them were too stupid to do the math on that one.

I'd caught Juan and Fatimah screwing a few times before—once in the kitchen where Fatimah had her naked ass pressed against the glass kitchen table while Juan, who didn't even have his pants all the way down, rammed himself into her, and another when they were out in the shed drinking some Crown Royal and smoking blunts. They were too high to notice me come through the door to put Enoch's tricycle away. All I ever did was shake my head and go on about my business. I had issues of my own with Niya, my little girlfriend from Vacation Bible School.

It was right after I graduated from high school, and I'd

signed up at church to teach Vacation Bible School. What the hell I had to offer the little children, I couldn't tell you, but, from time to time, I thought that maybe I could be a positive influence in somebody's life. I was eighteen, and Niya was twenty-two. She wasn't really that pretty to me, but I found myself attracted to her all the same. Her spirit was as free as mine.

We spent quite a bit of time talking to each other, and then one day while she was visiting me in my classroom, she leaned in and kissed me softly on the lips.

Suddenly, my tiny nipples rose to meet the fabric of my cotton blouse. "What did you do that for?" I asked offensively.

"Because I find your lips sexy and wanted to see how they felt against mine," she answered with just a hint of sass.

Blushing a little, I responded, "You could have at least waited until we were out of church."

"Yeah, you're right. I probably should have, but if I had done that, I might not have gotten a chance to see you surprised and *react* the way you did." She chuckled.

Well, that one little kiss eventually turned into the romance of the summer for me. I loved on this woman like Hershey's chocolate mixing with white milk, and it was good for me, until Niya told me she was leaving Atlanta to go away to DC. "You're leaving for good?"

"Torri, there is nothing here for me. I always hear about people trying to get to Hotlanta, and I don't understand what the big deal is. I've lived in this city all my life, and I need a change."

I was heartbroken that she didn't think enough of me to stay in Atlanta.

My mother had left me with Fatimah when I was eleven years old. It was Thanksgiving Day, and Fatimah had sent her to the store to get some more Brown 'n Serve rolls. Momma never came back, and, to this day, I don't give a damn about Thanksgiving Day or bread of any kind. And now after having experienced what I believed to be the love of a lifetime, I was being left behind again.

"You wouldn't stay here for me? I mean, I know I'm young and all, but I've got potential. I think I love you."

"That's just it. You *think* you love me. Tell me this, Torri. How many women have you been with besides me?"

"I've only been with one woman, and that's you."

"Exactly. Now, how many men have you been with?"

"Well, none actually. You were the first person I've ever had any feelings for."

Niya was a little annoyed with me. "Shit, you ain't even had a dick to know if you like it or not. Tell you what. Go out and get dicked down a time or two, and then let me know how you feel."

For the life of me, I couldn't understand why Niya was acting that way with me. She'd told me she loved me over and over again. Then, out of nowhere, she's acting like she doesn't want to be with me.

I walked over to her and tried to put my arms around her waist, but she pushed them away. "Niya, I don't get it. What have I done? Please, please tell me what I did wrong, so I can fix it . . . so I can fix us."

She stared at me as if she were breathing in my presence one last time. "I have to go. If you ever finally get some dick and realize you don't like it, find your way to DC and maybe we can talk."

Two weeks later, I was sitting on the couch in the living room, and I saw Fatimah coming up the steps of the porch to the front door. She got the mail out the mailbox and hurried into the house. Plopping her five-foot eleven-inch frame down on the couch next to me, she pulled out a Newport and started digging in her purse for her lighter. "What's up, Toe-toe?" she asked. She gave me that nickname partly because it was part of my name but mainly because I had huge big toes.

Not being able to find her lighter, Fatimah got up, went over to the stove, and lit the burner. Careful to not let her braids dangle too close to the flame, she stuck the tip of the cigarette into the flame waiting for it to turn a bright orange. She took two quick draws and came back over to the sofa.

"Nothing much," I answered.

"Oh, OK. I'm gon' get right to the point. Uh, me and Juan got a place over in East Point, so we gonna be moving in there within the next few days. He wants you to come with us."

I was uneasy about that offer, but I really didn't have a choice. "That's cool. When do I have to be ready?"

Taking another draw from the Newport and blowing the smoke toward the ceiling, she said, "He'll tell you all about that when he gets in this evening."

Juan came in around nine that night, went straight into the bedroom with Fatimah, and closed the door. I had been sleeping on the couch since I'd discovered them humping on my bed. I had this thing about sleeping in somebody else's juices.

Within the first ten minutes of him being in there, I heard nothing but Fatimah moaning. My guess was that he was eating her pussy, because he was a talker whenever he was stroking. "Yeah, baby, whose pussy is this? What's my name? Feel good to you, don't it? I'm writing my name all in this pussy!"

All of that was unnecessary to me, but you better not

let Fatimah know that. For every question, she had an answer.

"It's your pussy, daddy! Oh, Juan, Juan! Feels good, baby. Feels real good," she would shriek.

Resting my head against the back of the sofa, I turned up the TV with the remote control and continued watching *Good Times*.

Five minutes later, the door opened and Fatimah came out with nothing on. "Juan wants to talk to you now."

I was a bit confused as to why she would come out the room naked like that. "What?"

Fatimah was noticeably uncomfortable. "Come on in here. He wants to talk to you." She reached for her robe on the back of the door.

"OK."

As I approached the door, there was the faint smell of funk and ass in the room. I slid back out and grabbed the Money Blessing. Two pumps took care of that.

"Fatimah, I—"

Just then, my aunt closed the door, leaving me in there with Juan, who was laying there with his dick in his hand.

Standing with my back pressed against the door, I folded my arms and did all I could to not let my eyes rest on him. "What's up, Juan?"

"Aw, you know what's up, shawty. Come on over here and have a seat next to me."

He was right. I did know what was up, and I never thought Fatimah would allow me to be put in this position. My heart still had a hole in it from my issue with Niya, and now my aunt's high-natured brother-in-law wants me to fuck him.

I walked over to the bed but refused to sit down. His

dick was the size of a slim can of Michelob Ultra. I'd never seen a dick before, but if they all looked like this one, then I might be interested in doing a little sumthin'-sumthin'.

"What's this about, Juan?"

Next to the bed was a big jar of Vaseline, and judging by the glistening film around his rod, he'd been making pretty good use of it. "You like this?" he asked, grasping himself with the palms of his hands.

I didn't answer him.

Juan removed his hands and rested back on his elbows, his thing at full attention. "Timah told you we was movin', right?"

"Yeah, she did."

"Well, I figured you wouldn't want to be left out in the cold, so I wanted to see what you'd be willin' to do to keep a roof over your head."

Juan knew I had nowhere else to go, and I couldn't believe Fatimah was letting him put me up to this. Crying like a baby wasn't going to do me any good, and trying to run to get help wasn't going to change things either.

"Juan, I . . ."

"You what, Torri?"

I didn't know what I was supposed to do or say. Fucking him was most definitely out of the question. I wasn't about to lose my virginity to this greasy-ass nigga. "I'm on my cycle, Juan."

"Shit, girl, you think I'm scared of a little blood?"

I was hoping he was. I took two steps back from him. I felt the tears forming. "Juan, what is it that you want me to do?"

Obviously irritated with me, Juan demanded, "I need you to get over and do somethin' to this dick to make me even consider lettin' you move in with us. You ain't got no job. You ain't bringin' no kind of money in here, and you ain't cookin' shit that everybody else can eat."

I was a vegetarian.

"So the way I see it," he explained, "you got to do somethin' to earn your keep. Now get over here and show big daddy what you got."

I slowly walked over to the bed, knelt down, and brought my face close to his dick. Taking a whiff, it smelled a bit pissy to me. When I extended my jaws wide enough for it to enter my mouth, I wanted to choke. My lips slid easily over the greased stick as I heard Juan sigh. The muscles in my mouth contracted with a sucking motion that sent jolts through his groin.

Disgusted by the thought of blowing my aunt's piece, I did what I needed to do make sure I kept a roof over my head.

Later in the night, after I had thrown my guts up, I sat on the couch and wondered if I'd be able to handle fucking Juan whenever he wanted me to, and after a few hours of soul-searching, I realized I didn't want that.

Fatimah's purse was sitting on the kitchen counter; I knew she had just cashed her paycheck because she always bought a case of Icehouse beer, two pounds of steamed shrimp, and a carton of cigarettes on payday. I got most of my belongings together and packed them in two plastic shopping bags. Not caring about the fallout from me stealing her money, I took the remaining two hundred dollars from the inside pocket of her purse and stuck it inside the 38DD cup of my bra.

I could be a lot of things with my life, but a cocksucker wasn't going to be one of them. I hopped on the bus toward downtown, where I would catch the Greyhound to Washington, DC.

* * *

The first person I saw when I walked into the DC terminal was Earl. He stuck out like a sore thumb among the dingy vagrants in the big open space. Standing there watching the arrival boards, Earl cut his eyes at me when he thought I wasn't looking. It was late July, but he was holding it down in a nice khaki suit with a yellow silk tie pressed against a beige and yellow striped shirt. His pleasant fragrance overpowered the stale, musty odor of the bus station, and I knew that whoever he was waiting on had to be luckiest person in the world.

"Excuse me," he said as I tried to swiftly walk past.

I hadn't brushed my teeth since before leaving Atlanta, and I smelled worse than a funky onion. God knows I was too ashamed to say anything back to him. I knew he was talking to me, but I kept on walking. "Excuse me, Redbone."

Yes, I was a redbone, but I didn't care too much for people reminding me of it. "What you say?" I asked, snapping my head back around at him.

Earl strolled over to me with a swagger I'd only seen in Morris Chestnut, and, from that moment on, I was taken. "I didn't mean to be disrespectful, but I wanted to say hello to you."

Now, if you have ever wondered what real money looked like—and I'm not talking about Benny, Andy, and Abraham—all you had to do was look at Earl. His nails were manicured with clear nail polish and filed in perfectly straight lines. On his right wrist, he wore a bracelet that had about five rows of ice in it, and on the other, he donned a Rolex surrounded in even more diamonds. His tie clip and cufflinks were encrusted in diamonds too.

Man, if I had just one of them, I'd be set for life. "Hello," I offered reluctantly.

"That's better," he said. "What you all frowned up for? You walking around here like somebody stole your bike."

I couldn't help but laugh at his silly ass. It was the first time I'd smiled in weeks. "No one has stolen my bike." I chuckled. "I just don't like to be called that."

"Called what?"

"What you said."

"What did I say?"

"Negro, puh-leeze. You know what you called me."

"OK, I apologize. What's your name then?"

I didn't know this man from Adam, but I wanted to know him. No other man like him had ever crossed my path, and I didn't want to take my eyes off him. "It's Torri . . . Torri Banks."

He extended his hand for me to shake it, but I couldn't trust this stranger I didn't want out of my sight.

"Rule of thumb, when someone offers to shake your hand, you should welcome the gesture. That's just good business practice. It breaks the ice. My name is Earl . . . Earl Dixon."

With my hands deep in my pockets, I thought about what I had to lose by shaking this man's hand. Nothing. I had nothing to lose. So I extended my hand into his and said, "Nice to meet you, Earl."

"Now that's what I'm talking about. What's a beautiful girl like you doing in a place like this?"

Sometimes I wondered how much it took out of a person to ask a dumb question. I was in the bus station with bags. My breath reeked like I'd been eating horse shit, and I smelled like a fucking toilet.

"Einstein, I just got in from Atlanta."

"Here to see family?"

"No."

"Friends?"

"No."

"Oh, you in school?"

Mr. Dixon was getting on my last nerve. "No, I'm not in school. I'm just up here to chill for a while."

"Oh, OK. I can dig that." Earl glanced down at his watch as the bus from Philly pulled up. "Look, I'm actually here to pick up a friend of mine. She and I are going to go and have a bite to eat after we leave here. Care to join us?"

I had fifty dollars in my bra. With that, I had to eat and find somewhere to live. The only thing I knew about DC was, the president lived there, and somewhere within its streets lived Niya. I had nothing to lose. Right?

Earl:

The Catch of the Century

When I first laid eyes on Kimona, I knew she'd become very valuable to me in business and in bed. She and I shared the kind of connection only husbands and wives share, and coming from a professional ho, that was something special. Yes, I said it. Kimona's a ho, and she'll probably agree with me. Shit, she'll even go as far as to say she's damn good at it, and that's why she makes the kind of paper she does. I got plenty of women at Allure who are definitely gritting on her, but as far as I'm concerned, that only makes them try harder and gets more money for the business.

On this particular day, I'd given my driver the day off and was at the Greyhound station to pick up Chauncey, this girl I personally recruited from Philly. I'd offered to fly her to DC, but she said she was afraid of flying and felt more comfortable on the bus.

While waiting around in the station for her bus to arrive, I couldn't help but look around to see if there were any new prospects wandering around.

Just as I was becoming disappointed with the pickings, my eyes fell upon Torri as she walked through the door. Holding two plastic white shopping bags, she had on a pale blue halter-top and a pair of blue jeans that hugged every curve she had. In my mind, I envisioned her wrapping those long legs of hers around my waist as she pressed her wet pussy against my groin. Torri had dark brown eyes that seemed to look right through you, and the thought of her gazing at me with her ass spread across my groin while she had me relaxed against the sheets made my shit hard as a rock.

When Chauncey walked in from the platform, just about every head in the place whipped around. Her white, skin-tight, fleece sweatsuit stuck to her body, wet from sweat accumulated from sitting on a hot bus for four hours. She had a white bandana tied around her head, jet black hair dropping just past her shoulder tips. The zipper of her jacket opened up to just beneath her breast, which proudly displayed her stage name, "Ice," in an intricate tattoo.

As Chauncey walked through the terminal, I saw men, women, and children trying to catch a glimpse of the pink thong that sat raised above the waistband of her pants. Even Torri's eyes lit up, and that's when I realized I just might be on to something.

We had dinner at Phillips Seafood down by the Southwest Waterfront, and while I wasn't really that hungry, it gave me an opportunity to spend some time with the ladies to see what I was working with.

Chauncey knew what was up, but Torri was a different deal. I hadn't had the chance to talk to her about the business yet. She was a little too quiet for me, and I wasn't sure how I was going to get her to loosen up.

"So, Chauncey," I began, "tell me a little bit about yourself. We didn't get a chance to talk much the other night at the club."

This girl was sitting at the table working the hell out of some crab legs with her sculptured nails. The waitress had brought her some utensils to use, but she acted like they were going to hold her back.

"Well, whatcha wanna know?" she asked, cracking the claw from the crab leg.

Amazed at her skills, I kept it simple for her. "You been to college?"

"Naw, shit. I barely got my GED. Once I finished with that, I knew college wasn't gonna be for me."

"I see. Got any kids?"

"Two, but they with they daddy."

I hated prying in people's lives, but when it came to the girls that worked for me, I made it my business to know them, so I wouldn't have any surprises. "Oh, OK. Um, are you two . . . I mean do you . . . well, you know—"

"If you askin' me if I'm still fuckin' him, the answer is no. That nigga and his little-ass dick can't do nothin' for me. I pay child support, and I see them maybe once a month."

"Alrighty then. So why do you want to work for Allure?"

Chauncey, dipping a huge chunk of crabmeat into a bowl of drawn butter, inhaled and then let out a light belch. "Honestly, you asked *me* to come work for *you*. I was fine where I was. On a good night, I was bringing in between five and ten grand. Now I sure as hell hope you can do better than that, or else I'll have my happy ass on the bus right back to Philly."

Shit. Five to ten gees a night? The only girl who was making that kind of money at Allure was Kimona, and it had taken her a while to get to that level. She would have a fucking fit if I brought somebody in off the street making loot like that right off the bat. Seemed like Chauncey just might be getting her ass back on that bus after all.

"Dayum, girl. You carryin' it like that?"

"Hell, yeah. I'm the top dawg at The Orchid."

"Can you prove it?"

Chauncey raised up from her plate and gave me a look like I only expected from Dee when I asked her to show me the books or something.

"Dude, what I look like? I don't be standing on stage handing out receipts and shit. I makes mine. Best believe that."

I knew how I could get to her. "OK, that's nice to know, but do they offer you full health, dental and vision benefits?"

"Naw, they don't."

"What about an apartment?"

"Naw, nothing like that. I can handle my own shit. Just pay me my bills, and I got the rest."

During this whole time, I had my eye on Torri. The only thing she ordered was a bowl of lobster and crab soup and a glass of water with lemon. I know she heard everything Chauncey and I were discussing, but she never interrupted. Her manners were shocking, and she even had the nerve to have a slight elegance to her. She wasn't nothing like this rough-ass, might-a-been-a-convict in front of me.

"Chauncey, my girls get paid, quite well, I might add, and all their needs are taken care of. The kind of money you talking about comes in time."

Chauncey miraculously stopped eating for a minute. "You playin' me, right?"

Adjusting myself in my chair, I leaned in close to where she could hear me. "Look, I'm going to keep it real. When I saw you shooting lemons out your pussy across the room, I was impressed. It takes mad skills to do some shit like that. I've got clients who'll pay top dollar to see some shit like that. Work for Allure, and let me show you what a business is really all about. As a bonus, I'll even pay your child support for you so you can have your money to yourself."

"Whatchasay? You gonna pay my child support for me? I ain't nevah heard of no shit like that. You must want Ice pretty freakin' bad, mo'fucker."

Licking my lips and giving her my notorious I-know-I'm-the-shit-I'm-gonna-make-you-love-me grin, I said, "I really do. I want you just that bad."

Tossing back her third Corona, Chauncey shook her head in agreement. "Bet. It's done."

I took Pennsylvania Avenue back to Allure, so I could drop off Chauncey. As soon as we got in the car, she pulled out a stick of Doublemint and slid it between her glossy lips.

Once the gum had gotten good and moist, it started. *Clack! Pop! Clack! Pop!*

Chauncey was looking out the window of my S550 Mercedes Benz like a typical tourist. Pointing at everything from monuments to street vendors, she truly made me rethink what I'd gotten myself into.

Dee didn't have time to school anybody on etiquette, and I sure as hell wasn't about to. I shouldn't have been surprised, though. I had found her in the bottom of the ghetto doing everything but a ho stroll, so I had to deal with it.

Because she was instantly jealous of anyone who had more tricks than she, Kimona was most likely going to eat her alive anyway.

As for me, I couldn't help but hear *cha-ching* every time I thought of that popping-shit-out-the-pussy thing. *Dayum*. That trick alone was going to have clients beating down the doors of Allure. Talk about a brotha gettin' paid!

We pulled up to Sixteenth and K in the middle of rush hour traffic. Perry, the doorman, reached for the front passenger door, but Chauncey had already released the lock and started getting out the car. I stayed where I was because I still had to drop off Torri.

Turning to face the backseat, I said, "This will only take a minute. I want to make sure Chauncey gets settled in."

Sitting in the back seat, Torri hadn't uttered a word since we'd picked up Chauncey. Like I said, she was too quiet for me, and, usually, those are the ones you have to watch. "It's cool. I'm enjoying the sights."

"Why don't you come sit up here, so I can give you a personal tour before I take you to your destination?"

Torri flashed thirty-two of the most perfect teeth I'd ever seen. "No, thanks, I'm fine back here. It's nice to have this kind of attention. Makes me feel important." She giggled.

I was down for the little game. She was really a cutie. "OK then, if that's what you want." Whipping out my cell phone, I continued, "Let me make a quick phone call, and we'll be on our way."

Dee didn't like me bringing strip club girls into Allure, but I thought they brought another perspective into the place. What a bitch wouldn't do for a dollar was the way I rolled, when it came to that. A woman willing to work her clit against a metal pole or work her groin against mechanics, landscapers, and factory workers who hadn't been home to shower would do anything for money. Besides, I wanted her to see Chauncey blow those damn lemons!

"Yeah, Dee, the girl from Philly I was telling you about is on her way up."

"I know. I saw her on the monitor. She's on the elevator with Brandy."

"Good. Take good care of her for me and keep her as far from Kimona as possible."

"Why? You already see a problem?"

"A potential one. I'll tell you about it when I get back. I've got an errand to run. Oh, and by the way, send Brandy out for a bag of lemons."

"What?"

"Just do it, girl. I'll see you later."

One of the most beautiful thoroughfares in the nation's capital is Rock Creek Parkway. It snakes along the backside of DC, taking you past the very edge of Georgetown, around the back of the Lincoln Monument, and whisks you along the Tidal Basin. Following it north will land you in upper Northwest DC, past the zoo and Connecticut Avenue, and following it south will dump you out at the Potomac. With my driver behind the wheel, I had seduced many women in the backseat while driving along the parkway, and today wasn't going to be any different. It simply meant I had to be a little more creative with my strategy.

I was able to point out different landmarks as we made our way north in the forty-five plus minutes that Torri and I had been riding. The entire time, I was conscious of her every move, thanks to the rearview mirror.

By the time we reached the zoo, I could tell she wasn't listening to me. To be perfectly honest, the northern end of the parkway was the most boring, so I turned the car around and headed back south.

"Is there anything in particular you want to see?"

Staring out the window, Torri replied, "No, nothing in particular. I'm just enjoying the peace and quiet. This really is a beautiful city."

"Oh, you haven't seen anything yet. I'm taking you back toward the city so I can really show you what we got."

Never making eye contact, Torri answered, "That's fine with me."

As we approached The Kennedy Center, I decided to switch things up and get a little personal with her. "Are you staying here with friends?"

"No, I'm not."

I stopped at the red light thinking about where I was going to take her next. "You got a hotel room or something?"

"No, I don't."

The one thing I noticed about Torri was that she only answered what she was asked and never offered anything more. In my line of business, that was important because you never knew who you were talking to, and many of my clients didn't want to hear about the girls' personal lives. In fact, some didn't want to talk at all.

Instead of continuing down past the back of the Lincoln Memorial, I pulled onto Constitution Avenue and found a parking space. "So you don't have anywhere to go while you're here?" I asked, turning the car off.

"Not really. I ran away. I hopped on the first bus that would get me as far from Atlanta as possible."

I turned around in my seat. "Are you in some kind of trouble? If you tell me a little about what's going on, I may be able to help."

Finally making eye contact with me, Torri got me with those eyes. "Look, Mr. Dixon, I—"

"Please call me Earl."

"All right, Earl. I was living with my aunt. Her sleazy-ass boyfriend wanted me to suck his dick and do whatever else he desired in exchange for somewhere to live. I crept some loot from my aunt's purse and got the hell out of Dodge."

So much for a new employee. Torri wasn't going to be able to handle it. "I see. In essence, you have nowhere to go."

"You got it. Let me ask you a question, though."

"Go right ahead."

Torri sat up in her seat. "Are you a professional pimp?"

I couldn't help but laugh out loud, because she was right. But no one had ever blurted it out like that before.

"I prefer not to be called that. I'm a businessman who profits from making my clients' fantasies come true. If that means that sex is involved, then my staff and I make it happen."

"Where do you get your girls from?"

"Uh, I have girls from New York, Boise, L.A., Phoenix, *Philly*. All over, actually."

"Any from Atlanta?"

Chuckling again, I softly said, "No, I don't have any young ladies from the A-T-L."

"Oh."

Torri kept looking through the window, I guess, to make sure no one was following us. I needed her to chill.

"I have an idea. We've been cooped up in this car for a

minute, and I know you must need to stretch those sexy long legs of yours. Let's get out and take a walk."

"I would like that," she responded. "On one condition, though."

"And what's that?"

"You have to let me stop at one of the vendors and get a pack of gum. I don't want to run you off with my breath."

"I noticed that back at the bus station, and it didn't make me run away then." I laughed.

"Oh, you got jokes. That's why I haven't had too much to say."

"I figured as much, and I can respect that."

I walked over to one of the stands and got her a pack of Dentyne. I watched her unwrap two pieces and discreetly place them in her mouth.

For as long as we were talking, I never noticed her gum. *Wow,* I thought. That was a first for me.

We walked to the Vietnam Memorial, where I gave Torri a brief introduction to its history. She rubbed her fingertips along some of the engraved names, and when we reached the end, she stopped and read the information at the end of the path.

"Do you mind me asking how old you are?"

"No, I don't mind. I'm eighteen."

"Get the fuck outta here! You're kidding."

Blushing slightly, she nodded. "No, I'm not. I graduated from high school a couple of months ago."

"You act more mature than some twenty-five-year-olds I know."

"Thank you."

Approaching the steps of the Lincoln Memorial, my cell phone rang. "Yeah."

It was Dee. "Earl, where the hell you at?"

"I'm still out and about. What's up?"

"Uh, you got us sitting here waiting for you with this damn bag of lemons."

"Ohhh, shit, that's right. I forgot all about that. I'm kinda in the middle of something and can't get away. Where's Chauncey?"

"She's in her apartment. Earl?"

"Yeah?"

"I don't like her. She's too fucking ghetto for me. She came in here asking for fans and incense. And that fucking gum!"

"I know, Dee, I know. Just trust me on this one. Give me a couple of hours, and I'll show you what I mean." Glancing down at Torri as she watched the Washington Monument's image in the Reflecting Pool, I whispered to Dee, "I think I might have something else to balance all of this out."

"I hope so, because she might have to go."

"Just trust me."

I loosened my tie and took it off. Folding it and placing it in my pocket, I took a seat next to Torri on the steps. "What's on your mind? You seem to be off somewhere else."

Pulling her long brown hair around her shoulders and putting it in a ponytail, she said, "I came here to look for someone. My friend Niya."

"OK. Any ideas where she might be?"

"No, I don't. For most of the summer, she was my lover."

Aw shit! I hit the jackpot. "Your lover?"

Torri turned to me. "Please don't judge me. You don't know me."

"Hey, hey. Do you actually think I'm the type to judge somebody, with what I do? Come on now."

"I was just making sure. You know how people can get."

"Well, you don't have to worry about that with me."

Tears began to well up in her eyes. "Niya was my first sexual experience with a man or woman. Juan's nasty ass was a one-time thing. I'm not going to say I didn't like it. It was simply something I didn't want to do." She sniffled. "One minute shit with Niya was cool, and the next she was calling it off, saying I needed more experience and that I didn't know anything about love."

"I see."

"I haven't had a chance to prove to anyone who I am or what I can do. Everybody that should love me keeps leaving me. I know I got skills."

Suddenly Torri's eyes glazed over, and then it started. "One night Niya surprised me and came to bed with a strap-on. It looked so fucking good on her. While I was lying on my side watching her stroll toward me, I imagined that dick in my mouth and didn't think about anything being wrong with that. The closer she got to me, the more my pussy throbbed and the wetter my mouth became. She stopped with it pointing directly in my face, and before I knew it, I reached for it with my mouth open wide. If I could have swallowed it, I would have.

"After I finished, Niya climbed into the bed, rested on her knees, and then asked me to spread open my legs. I dropped open my thighs, and, with her right fore and index fingers, she massaged my jewels from top to bottom. She entered me gently as my body entered a realm it had never visited. Measuring my motions against my moans, Niya found a moment in which to introduce my body to the penetration of a man's organ. My natural reaction was to move my hips in sync with hers as I wrapped my lips around her breasts dangling just above my body. Her excitement was obvious by the way her circular movements turned into pelvic thrusts that made me scream.

Right when I thought I was going to explode, she pulled out and dropped down to put her tongue against my rock-hard clit. Then, without warning, I came. My juice sprayed her face like a stream of water from a spray nozzle. I was a little embarrassed, but she made me feel comfortable by licking her lips and sensually wiping her face against my groin."

At this point I'd nutted all in my pants. I pulled my shirt from inside and stretched it over my zipper. Shit, I thought I was the one supposed to be doing the seducing. Torri brought a brother to his knees with that, and I immediately knew who she would great be for. Sweat was running down my forehead. I had a kazillion questions for her, but there was one that was most important. "So are you telling me you can shoot cum across the room?"

"Well, yeah, I guess so."

To hell with Chauncey and the pussy-popping lemons. I had just landed the catch of the century.

Torri:

Kimona and Lady Dee

Two of the simplest and most scandalous bitches I know are Kimona and Lady Dee. I have never seen women fight over who's going to run a cat house. They are constantly going at it like two old alley cats. Don't get me wrong. It's profitable as hell and has phenomenal clout with all the high-profile clients it has running up through there. I just don't understand why Earl thinks that either of those two idiots can keep it like that. Lady Dee doesn't want Kimona to have any more than her, and Kimona doesn't want Lady Dee to have any of it.

On the real, Lady Dee is a control freak, and she's nasty. I heard about her screwing the guys she wanted to have working in here, and she's been letting them do just that without Earl's permission. I know this because one of them, Hot Chocolate, actually, is fucking the mayor's wife, Carlotta. What kills me is Kimona and Dee are so caught up in trying to destroy one another that they don't THINK. The mayor has crazy security with him all the time; it's their job to always know what's going on around him . . . all the time. They also make sure they know what's going on with his family and whatever the hell they're doing, so that nobody gets caught up in some shit that could cause a scandal.

Ever since that Marion Barry episode, security doesn't take any chances. Marcel, the top dog in charge of the mayor's safety, was up here the first day Carlotta came in for a little recreation. By the time he left, he had her credit card receipt, all the tapes from the monitors, and the sheets she'd fucked Hot Chocolate on. Brandy's crooked ass was no joke. Ain't no telling what they paid her for all that shit. All I know is that the mayor didn't have room for a scandal. Even with him as my client, they never took chances.

Mayor Roderick Gibson had a dick that, when erect, extended down to the tip of his knee cap. He loved when I played with it like it was a piece of PLAY-DOH or something. I pulled at it, stretched it, wiggled it, ran the tip of it across my face, and, on occasion, provided warmth for it between my breasts. Marcel and his crew weren't allowed inside Allure while Roderick was there, but he was always miked up in case there was ever a problem. Dee was so busy trying to be the smartest bitch in the joint that she let a little detail like that slip past her.

I hate Kimona. Yes, she's beautiful and has mad skills. Yeah, we kicked it once, but it didn't change my opinion of her. She walks around this place as if she owns it and doesn't give a damn who knows it.

I am the only woman in Allure that Earl hasn't fucked, and he's not ever going to get any of this. One thing that is true about the two of us is that he and I talk like brother and sister. I can go to him with anything, at any time, and he is able to come to me with anything. He was the first person to ever tell me that I had class. I mean, coming from my background and having been around certain shit, that was a true compliment.

Earl trusted me enough to give me some of his biggest clients, so that's how I ended up with the mayor. I never asked a lot of questions, and I typically only spoke when spoken to. I respected other people's privacy, and I expected them to do the same in return. I guess that could be why Earl and I get along so well. I don't pop my gum, and I know how and when to be a lady. Quite unusual for the less popular of the joint, I was personally recommended by the boss for certain assignments, and furthermore, I never had to pimp myself to get him to do it.

During Chauncey's first week, I had the opportunity to see what all the noise was about. Earl was geeked because this girl could shoot full-sized lemons from that hole at the bottom of her ass. I burst his bubble when I told him any woman could blow a lemon outta her ass if she tried, especially if she's experienced childbirth. It's simply the air from the diaphragm pushed down through the vaginal cavity. Chauncey had managed to make entertainment out of it. Shit, if she did it hard enough, she could probably blow out a candle too.

Earl didn't care what did what and how it got where. All he wanted her to do was entertain his clients. Dee had been videotaping the stunt so she could see how folks were going to react. I can honestly say it backfired because a couple of the clients were completely turned off by it, and some others, with their beyond-intellectual asses, wanted to *study* her.

Definitely, Chauncey was making nice money, but she got greedy too fast and wanted more before she had even been there a month. Now, you know for damn sure Kimona wasn't having that, and surprisingly, neither was Dee. Within three weeks, Lady Dee pulled the plug on Chauncey and sent her ass right on back to Philly.

Kimona:

Tricks of the Trade

Earl must've been smoking crack when he found Chauncey. He brought the Queen of the Ghetto to an establishment of nothing but pure class. She had a bandana to match every outfit she wore, and her thong always sat on top of her waistbands. As bad as I hate to say it, Dee tried to teach her some manners. I mean she *really* tried. She did. The first thing that had to go was the gum. I'm a gum chewer and can sometimes get carried away with the popping and cracking, but this hooch had me beat.

All of the girls in Allure were pictures of perfection. Nice round asses and curvaceous hips. Succulent lips and flawless skin. Beautiful toes and manicured nails. During the brief time frame when Dee was trying to work with Chauncey, she discovered that ol' girl was missing her second toe on her right foot. Obviously, that ruled out the mandatory flip-flops in the sauna, and it ruined the fantasy whenever a client saw her. Could you imagine her wearing those damn things and tossing the right shoe across the room every time she took a step?

Unh-unh. That was so unattractive and simply wasn't going to happen at Allure. The clients wanted perfection, and we were paid extremely well to give it to them.

Chauncey was gritting on me the minute she laid eyes on me. She looked me dead in the eye and then had the nerve to roll her eyes. If it wasn't for the fact that physical catfights were against the rules and were grounds for immediate eviction from the house, I would've scratched the bitch's eyes out. I tried, from time to time, to help her get used to the house rules, but the heifer kept on getting nastier with each day. She was just straight-up shitty. So that's why I let her dig her own grave. Teach her stank ass a lesson.

One morning during lineup I noticed that Chauncey was wearing a see-through negligee she obviously didn't get from Dee. Allure had a strict requirement that its girls could only wear items from a pre-approved wardrobe that we called "the closet." If there was an outfit in there that you knew you could rock, your opinion about it didn't mean shit. It still had to pass Dee's inspection, and there was no guarantee that she was going to agree with your choice.

I could tell what Chauncey had on was some mammy-made shit because the fur around the collar and the sleeves was knotty. Then the thong she had on didn't fully cover her in the front while it exposed the worst violation of all the house rules: a bush.

Not one of us was allowed to have hair on our pussies for a slew of reasons. The first was because it held odor; the second was because it could and would hold lice and/or crabs; the third was because it looked nasty; fourth, it left a DNA trail; and five, it could get in the teeth and mouth of clients who liked to eat pussy.

There was a groomer specifically paid to inspect and

shave us every two weeks. It was a bit humiliating at first, but after a while, we got used to it. Each of us had our own signature cuts or styles, and it spoke volumes about our class.

The top girl never got in the lineup. She was considered a surprise, for those willing to pay to be with the best. So, ***I*** never had to go.

This particular morning, though, I fell in with the rest of them because I'd seen Chauncey in the hallway proudly sporting her bush. "Hey, girl," I said, strutting past her to take place up front.

I knew the bitch wasn't going to speak. Everybody else did, but she didn't say shit. Peeping from around the girls standing beside me, I gestured with my forefinger for her to come to me. At first, she rolled her eyes, yet again, at me.

"Oh, you think you too good to speak?" I asked.

Surprisingly, Chauncey reluctantly responded. "No, I don't, but I do refrain from talking to skank hoes that spread gossip about me."

Refrain? Did she know such a word? Did she even know what it meant? Could she spell it? I stepped out of line and casually waltzed my happy ass over to her. It took everything within me to keep from bitch-slapping her ass Southeast DC style. Because I had big plans for Allure, I had to maintain my cool. "Chauncey, I'm not spreading any gossip about you. I merely wanted you to know you need to get that nappy dugout shaved off your pussy before Dee sees it. It's a violation."

"Fuck you, bitch. I ain't shaving shit."

With that, I didn't give a damn what happened to her.

Dee walked in quickly and cut her eyes at everybody in the lineup but stopped right smack in front of Chauncey. "What the hell?" she posed to herself. Looking down at Chauncey's attire, she couldn't help but see it. "Uh, did you miss your appointment with Regina this week?"

Making motions to put her chewing gum between her teeth and gums, Chauncey replied, "No, I didn't. I wasn't aware it was mandatory."

"Uh, yes, it is. Where'd you get this cheap-looking get-up you wearing?"

Appearing slightly offended, she commented, "I got it from home. My boyfriend gave it to me a couple of years ago."

"Right, and it looks like it. You need to return to your apartment and get yourself together. There is no way in hell you're going to see anybody looking like that." As Chauncey began walking away, Dee continued, "Oh, yeah, spit out the gum."

Wow. Busted like that in front of everybody. Ahee-hee for that ho.

Torri is a totally separate issue. Earl wants me to have her as my assistant, and, like I said about when he met Chauncey, he must have been smoking rocks. I have set aside mad loot to make Allure all mine . . . ALL mine. I don't need some new bitch coming in trying to get next to me and keep an eye on me for Earl. I know Earl and Torri are pretty close, and that she's the only one of us he hasn't fucked. I was pissed off when he gave Torri the mayor. My pussy's got fire running through it, and Earl knows I would've set the mayor's dick ablaze. I guess the last thing he needed was someone like me having the mayor on lock. Earl knows the kind of shit I got; it only takes one time to get a nucca hooked on this. He did the right thing by giving the mayor to Torri, but when this whole thing is all over said and done, I'll be the one laughing all the way to the bank.

Torri brings in about five thousand more than me a week. That's because the Senator blows through here and leaves her a hefty-ass tip in addition to the services provided. All totaled, that one client nets Allure over seventy-five hundred dollars. The only three people who know what goes in that room are Torri, Earl, and the senator. The room is swept thoroughly for wires, bugs, and cameras.

Earl once caught Dee with a tape from Torri's room and immediately snatched it, furiously warning Dee he'd kill her if he ever found out Torri's room was being taped again. I know what she brings in because it's my business to know which one of these skanks is making me look bad. All I have to do is yank on Earl's dick a time or two and he'll tell me almost everything I want to know. Notice I said *almost*.

Typically, fees for our services range from around a measly two grand to the extravagant paper Torri brings in. For two gees, you can get your dick sucked with whipped cream, honey, jam, or whatever the client desires. Drop another thousand, and your girl will swallow. Four thousand and up is custom-tailored to each client's requests. That idiot that gave me the golden shower coughed up five grand for the books, and another five grand was paid directly to me. Dee didn't see everything as she claims, and it was simply none of her damn business what went on in my apartment. I knew Earl was going to side with me, and now the only thing I had to do was to show him Torri and I wouldn't be running Allure together.

Torri:

The Senator

Senator Rita Mabry, head of the United States Ethics Commission and graduate of Howard Law School, came to me on one of the loneliest and coldest days of my life.

I had been in DC and at Allure for a little over a year, and I still hadn't found Niya. In my spare time, I had gone to all of the HBCU homecomings in the area, scouted out all of the malls, gone to the hottest parties, and went to every club the area had to offer. I walked the open campuses of all the local colleges and universities in hopes of finding her and had not had any luck. I listened to PGC, KYS, and HUR, praying that she'd be on the radio giving a shout-out or something, but it never happened. On some of the weekends when I didn't have to work, I sat on the Mall and thought maybe she'd jog or walk by. I watched all the news channels and read all of the local newspapers, thinking maybe Niya would be featured somewhere. I even broke down and asked Earl if he could help me find her, and I was surprised when he told me he'd do what he could.

"You don't have any idea where she could be?" he asked.

Whimpering slightly, I replied softly, "No, I don't. It's as if she disappeared into thin air."

"Torri, something you need to know about DC is that it is very easy to simply vanish in this city. I mean, you got northern Virginia and Maryland to contend with too. Have you tried those areas?"

"No, I haven't. Some days I get so disappointed that I want to give up and move on. Then when I go to bed at night, there she is . . . in my dreams. I have to find her, Earl." I started crying, pouring tears into the palms of my hands.

Earl pulled me to him and stroked my hand like a big brother. "It's going to be OK, honey. I promise."

Two days later I was summoned to the office by Dee. "What's going on with you, Torri?" She gestured for me to take a seat.

"Uh, nothing really. Just chillin' as usual." I was uneasy because Dee was known for that freaky shit on a whim. I was expecting her crew in any minute, and they would have their tools in tow. Next thing I'd know we'd be in the dungeon. I wasn't feeling up to all of that, but if that's what the boss wanted, then that's what I had to do.

"I see. Look, I have a client that came to us specifically requesting your services."

"Requesting me?" Nothing like that had ever happened to me. The mayor hadn't even come to me like that.

"Yeah. Are you familiar with politics in any way?"

"Not really."

"Good. She will be here around two this afternoon. Go back to your apartment and get yourself together."

"She?"

"OK, well, you really don't know anything about politics. Senator Mabry is one of the finest women in government, if I must say so myself. She's a heavy hitter and has major clout in this town. Earl knows you keep your mouth shut about everything, and that's really important here. As a matter of fact, security is doing a sweep of your room right now—at Earl's request. I don't even know what's going on in there, and that's a first."

"OK."

"I think you should know Earl has typically, in the past, denied us having this girl-on-girl thing. We've had a number of women coming in here for this shit, and he has wanted to stay away from that kind of drama. You know how y'all do," she said, checking her makeup in the mirror she kept in the top right desk drawer.

"Actually, no, I don't. Why don't you inform me?"

"No need. I don't think you're like that. The mayor thinks you walk on water, and with all his ranting and raving, it's hard to believe you're a dyke."

Offended but determined to keep my cool, I calmly asked, "Have I ever given you any reason to think I was such a thing?"

"Girl, you know Earl tells me everything. There are no secrets around here when it comes to employees. I know you handle the mayor to make your paper, and I ain't mad at you for it."

I didn't care about Dee calling me a dyke. I am what I am. What hurt was that Earl had betrayed me. He was the only person I trusted, and he treated that trust like concrete and walked all over it. Sure, I had a preference when it came to sex, but it was merely that. It was like being in an ice cream parlor. You see pralines and cream, but your preference is butter pecan—and it's not available. So you settle for the pralines and cream until you can get some butter pecan. Outside of the occasional demands from Kimona and some of the other girls, I never got a chance to dabble in what I really preferred. And, as far as having a friend in this place, that had gone straight to hell. I went to my room to cry but knew my tears would be wasted because the only person who would see them was me.

At three minutes till two, I was sprawled across my bed in a kelly green bra and thong set. I smelled of Coco Chanel with a light dusting of bronzing powder spread over my chest and shoulders. I pinched my cheeks to give myself some color and had been using cold compresses to get rid of the bags beneath my eyes. As usual, my makeup was flawless.

Normally, clients picked their girls out of the lineup, but this was a different scenario. Everything had been pre-planned, and I had been given specific instructions to wait in the bedroom of my apartment.

At five after two, I heard a key in the lock of the side door—the door we used only in case of an emergency. My heart began to beat unusually fast, and that was a feeling I wasn't accustomed to experiencing. Seconds later, I heard heels clicking tenderly against the hardwood floors, making their approach to the hallway leading to my bedroom. I sat up slightly in my bed and checked my hair in the mirror above my bed. The footsteps came one right after the other until they reached the closed door to my room.

Sliding myself toward the six down pillows resting against my headboard, the butterflies in my stomach fluttered faster and more intensely. As the doorknob turned, I wasn't sure if I wanted to close my eyes and be startled or leave them open and allow them to bulge from their sockets. I chose to close them and wait for the senator.

"Why are you sitting there with your eyes closed like you scared to see the boogey man?" a woman asked, chuckling.

We were into the first week of November, and the weather outside was brisk. Her presence brought a burst of cool air into the room that was quickly warmed by the rising temperature. My nipples were a little perky but calmed down after a few seconds.

When I opened my eyes, there was a silhouette of a woman in front of me with her back to me. Cloaked in a navy blue cape, I watched her take off her black gloves and place them on the dresser. I never spoke until spoken to but took direction all the same. As she lowered the hood of her cape, all I could see was salt and pepper locks hanging from the sides and back. She took off her cape and hung it on the back of the door.

"Cat got your tongue?"

Coyly, I answered, "No, ma'am."

"That's right." She laughed heartily. "Earl told me you were from the South. No need for those kind of pleasantries with me."

I couldn't help but laugh because she wasn't the first person to tell me that. That yes, ma'am-no, ma'am thing was something I dealt with most of my life. No matter who you spoke to in Georgia it was expected. "OK," I said.

I didn't count on being as nervous as I was. Here, in front of me, was a woman that seemed to be about twenty years older than me, and my job was to fulfill her fantasies.

Finally, the senator turned around and revealed one of

the most beautiful women I had ever seen. She had gray eyes with well-coiffed eyebrows. Her skin was the color of silky caramel and reminded me of the Sugar Daddies I used get from the corner store by Fatimah's house. She smelled of a fragrance I didn't recognize, yet it filled my room with an unmistakable aura of richness. Dressed in basic black—a black pinstriped suit with an ivory blouse beneath, she took a seat on the chaise lounge next to the bed. "So how are you?"

"I'm fine, and yourself?"

"I'm well. Thanks for asking," the senator replied. "If you don't mind me saying, you are absolutely beautiful."

"Thank you." I got up from the other side of the bed and walked over to the mini-bar. "Would you like something to drink?"

I felt her eyes piercing my flesh. "I'd like that. What do you have?"

"Well, I have three types of water—spring, flavored, and sparkling. I have three types of beer—Corona, Heineken, and Amstel Light. Uh, I have sodas—Coke, Diet Coke, Sprite, Ginger Ale, and Sunkist Grape. If you don't want any of that, I have milk, tea, or juice. And, of course, I can make you a cocktail or have one brought up for you."

"Wow." She smiled. "Let's keep it simple for you. I'll take some spring water for now."

Handing the water to her, I noticed a wedding band on her left ringer finger. "Are you comfortable? Is it too hot in here for you?" I walked back over to the bed and resumed my position.

The senator had a small gap between her teeth. Not a Lauren Hutton gap, but more like a Whoopi Goldberg one. "I'm comfortable. Just relax. I want to sit and talk with you for a while. We've got all evening."

"OK, if that's what you want."

Occasionally, the mayor would want to sit and talk for a while, so I was used to the conversation piece to this puzzle. But I wasn't sure what to expect next.

After nearly five hours of laughing and talking, the senator got up, walked over to the door to retrieve her cape. We hadn't touched, kissed or fucked. In all that time, we chatted about everything from Chanel to Tang. Reaching for her cape, she said, "You're a very intelligent young lady, Torri. Might I ask why you're working here in a place like this?"

Obviously, she had caught me way off guard. "Uh, wow." I knew there were no cameras or voice recorders, so I was able to speak freely. No one had ever asked me why I was at Allure or why I wanted to be at Allure—not even Earl. "Do you have a minute then? I don't mind telling you, but I don't want you to misunderstand me."

The senator reclaimed her seat in the chaise lounge. "You can take as long as you want. I've paid for your time for the entire evening. I was only leaving because I thought maybe you were tired of talking to me."

"No, no, no. I was enjoying the conversation. It's such a change from the others. The only person I've really ever talked to around here is Earl."

"So tell me, why are you here?"

I pulled a chenille throw from the edge of the bed and covered the bottom half of my body. The usual sirens of DC came from outside the window. Flicking tiny grains of lint from my beneath my nails, I reluctantly began my story. "My mother left me when I was a little girl, and I ended up staying with my aunt, who was willing to let her boyfriend pimp me for his own sexual purposes. In order for me to have somewhere to live, he wanted me to do to him whatever he asked. I ran away the first night it happened and got a bus to DC. At the bus station I bumped into Earl, and the rest is history."

Relaxed in the corner of her seat, the Senator asked, "So you've been intimate with Earl, too?"

Earl, too? How did she know about any of that? "No, I haven't. As far as I can tell, he's slept with everyone but me. He's more like a brother to me, I guess."

"Honey, Earl is a businessman before he's anything else. I respect your respect for him, but trust me when I say, Earl Dixon is about business. Come on, now, don't be naïve. Who else knows you're into women enough to entertain them and make good money from it?"

The senator had a point, and I was mad as hell at the fact that Earl had been telling all my business. "He told you about me? What did he say?"

"Whoa, Torri. Just calm down. He didn't say anything about you. Look, I just wanted some pleasant conversation with someone other than those nutcases on the Hill. Like I said, you're a bright girl, and it seems such a waste for you to be in this place. I wasn't expecting this."

I calmed myself and offered more conversation. "I came here to look for a friend of mine."

"Good luck in this town." She laughed.

"She . . ."

Without warning, the senator sat up in the chair. "Get dressed and come with me." She flung my robe toward me and walked out the bedroom.

I grabbed my jeans and a sweater and headed toward the front door of the apartment to only find she was standing by the side-door entrance.

"I never use the front door. For as long as I come here, I will never use the front door."

"OK."

The senator and I rode in her car along the Tidal Basin and on into Hains Point. Heading back out the park, she abruptly stopped and opened her door.

When she exited the car, I sat in my seat, waiting for her to come over to my side and open the door. Instead, she stood on her side of the vehicle and waited for me to get out. *Guess I'll open my own fucking door, then.* And I did. I got out and walked over to her.

The weather was freezing, but the beautiful view of Rosslyn at night made me forget all about it. "I've never seen this before," I uttered in amazement.

"I know. Most people haven't. This place used to be filled with folks trying to get their freak on. The city's been trying to clean it up for years. You can't even go down toward the back anymore."

"It's beautiful, but, uh, my ass is cold. Why are we out here?"

It took her a minute to get her thoughts together as she stood braving the chilled wind off the Potomac River. "I want to bring Allure down, and I'm going to need your help."

"What?"

"Listen, there's some stuff going on in there that I can't talk about right now. However, I will say that Earl, Dee, Brandy, and Kimona are all suspect at this point."

"Earl is a good guy, Senator. Now, those other two bitches? That's a different story. I don't trust them as far as I can see them. Dee is stealing business and money from Earl, and Kimona is just straight-up stealing. I'm not really sure what she's doing with it."

"Yeah, we've been investigating Earl and his wife for a while. There really isn't anything we can get him on, other than operating a brothel three blocks from the White

House. With that, he's got too many ways to take the spotlight off him. All he has to do is roll on Dee or Kimona."

"I thought prostitution was illegal. Isn't that what it is? We're selling sex, you know."

"It is highly illegal, but the Ethics Commission doesn't give a damn about Allure selling sex to sex-starved men. Earl is a man, as are the other members of the Ethics Commission. If anything, he'll get a slap on the wrist, a fine but no jail time. After the smoke clears, he'll likely open again under another name and then do it with a client list twice as long as his previous one because of all the free publicity the federal government will have given him. Men protect their own. It's pretty fucked up, but that's the way it is."

"So what's the point of doing this, if you already know the outcome?"

The senator pondered a moment, watching a plane coming in over the Potomac for a landing at Reagan National Airport. "How old are you?"

"I'll be twenty-one on my next birthday."

"OK. How long have you been working in this particular capacity at Allure?"

"Since I was eighteen."

"Tell me something—How old do you think Kimona and Dee are?"

Blowing my breath into the palms of my hands for quick heat, I said, "Um, Dee is thirty-two, from what I recall Earl telling me, and Kimona is twenty-five. I might not like them, but I will admit that they look really good for their ages."

"They should. Kimona just turned nineteen. Dee is a little older than that, but not much. She started working when she was around fifteen and retired a while ago to get that top job working for Earl."

"Wait, wait, wait. I don't understand. You're trying to say Kimona is underage?"

"That's exactly what I'm saying. Dee is old enough now to where we can't do anything about her, but they did both falsify records to be able to work for Allure. What we're having trouble proving is whether or not Earl knew about it."

I wasn't sure what the fuck I was supposed to say. Kimona and Dee didn't act that young, but then again, maybe they did. "I'm still trying to figure this out, and you still haven't told me what it is you want me to do."

"Earl is reporting these ladies on payroll and even paying taxes on them, but they're not filing taxes at all. According to information that Earl has been submitting to the IRS, they're old enough to file taxes, and legally, they should be filing them. What's happening, though, is that neither of them is doing what the hell they're supposed to do as law-abiding citizens." She laughed. "I know you all get a hefty sum under the table. Shit, I know for a fact that Roderick leaves you at least a two- to three-thousand-dollar tip—taxpayer's money, of course. All of that is moot because Earl is and has been employing young girls to engage in paid sexual activity."

"You can't prove it, though."

"Well, now that I've talked to you, yes, I can."

"Huh?"

"You just told me you were eighteen."

Damn. I sure had. At this point, all I could do was hope that somehow I had fallen asleep and was in one of those dreams where all I had to do was wake up and this shit would be over. "Why are you coming to me?"

"You want to know how I really found out about you?"

"It would be nice."

"Roderick."

"The mayor? Oh, come on. You've got to be fucking kidding me. He's in on this?"

"Yes, he is, but you can't say anything to him or anybody else about it. It would ruin everything."

Shocked beyond belief, I was numb—and not from the cold. "I don't get this. You just met me like seven hours ago. How can you even come to me when you know I could run right back to the others and tell them what you're up to?"

"We don't have a lot of time with this. Allure has been under investigation for several months, and the Ethics Commission wants to raid it, like yesterday, and expose everybody who has ever fallen up in there. Now, do you think I can let that happen? Roderick is my boy. He and I go way back, and I'm not going to let his term be tarnished over a high-class cat house. Besides, you can't stand Kimona and Dee, so your ratting them out isn't going to be an issue."

Why me, Lord? Why me? "I'm sorry, Senator. I can't help you. Do you know how many lives you will destroy?"

Exasperated with my comments, she fired back, "Please don't tell me you give a damn about these people. They are using you, Torri."

"Well, so are you. Take me home, please," I demanded, wiping snot away from my frost-bitten nose. I began walking toward the car.

"I know where Niya is."

Just the sound of her name warmed the blood running through my veins, but that blood was now seeping out of my back because the Senator had thrown a dagger in it. I stopped in my tracks and glared into the night sky. How in the hell did she know anything about Niya? Turning around slowly toward her direction, I tearfully asked, "What do you mean?"

The senator, tiptoeing through the dampened earth, strolled over to me with the hood of her cape now covering her eyes. "I know who she is and where she is, but you've got to tell me you're on board with this."

"Yes, anything. I'll do anything if you're going to tell me where she is."

The Senator:

The Plan

I never went into this arrangement with Torri for the sex. Hell, I could get that from anywhere, but that night after I took her back to Allure, I wanted her. I waited for her to get out of the car. "You OK with this?" I asked.

"I'm going to have to be. Are you coming up, or is this the end of our evening?"

"That's up to you, Miss Lady."

"May I ask a question?"

"Anything," I answered.

"Are you gay, or are you just doing this for your political portfolio?"

Torri was entitled to ask that question.

"Yes, I am," I snickered.

"You're what?"

"Gay."

"I don't believe you. After all this, I simply don't believe you."

Sixteenth Street had calmed down tremendously for

the evening, and I knew that Paulette, my wife, had to work the late shift at the hospital. "I bet I can show you better than I could tell you."

Torri hopelessly stared as if she had no other choice but to be where she was. Then, with a bit of humor tossed in, she said, "If seeing is believing, then you need to show me what you got."

As soon as she turned the knob on the side door, I pushed her inside, slammed the door closed, turned her to me, and planted my lips firmly against hers. She didn't hold back, entangling my tongue with her wet, passionate grip. Gliding my hands along the path of hers, I met the tips of her fingers at the top of her zipper. We both raced to unzip her pants, and as I felt my fingers graze the smooth surface shielding her golden nugget, I grabbed her kisses—one right after the other—and exchanged them with strokes against her jewel.

As she squeezed my hands between her thighs, I thrusted them further into her pocket of her womanhood. Only interested in the size of her protruding clit, I moved the tips of my fingers against it as I felt it pulsating. My intention was to touch her and to feel her in my hands. The rushing waters from her well covered my hands, and it was then that I knew I needed to have her body next to mine.

"Come to the bed with me," I asked gently.

The way our interlude was supposed to work involved Torri getting on top of me and saturating every inch of my body with her. Instead, I took charge.

Leading her to the bedroom, I began unbuttoning my blouse with one hand while I held her hand with the other. Once inside, we both undressed until we were naked.

Like two schoolgirls, we stood there gazing at one another. My eyes absorbed every inch of her body as I contemplated what part of her I was going to tackle first. "Are you going to make me come and get you?" I joked.

"Only if you promise to tell me I've been a bad girl," Torri whined, her thumb in her mouth.

I was amazed by the fact she knew how to appeal to the dominatrix in me. A little role-playing always made me horny, and I was more than interested in what I had dropped seventy-five hundred dollars for.

I went into the pocket of my cape and pulled out a black silk scarf. Torri's eyes followed every move I made until I disappeared behind her slender body. I could feel her magnetic energy, as my nipples gently touched the raised hairs on her back. Slowly, I lifted my hands and placed the scarf around her eyes, pulling it until I was certain she couldn't see. With my hands around her waist, I guided her to the bed where she took a seat.

"Do you have a tie or some old—"

As if the lines were programmed in her head, Torri said, "You'll find everything you need in the nightstand."

"OK." I opened the nightstand drawer, and, amongst all the other goodies in there, I saw four sets of handcuffs.

While her legs dangled off the side of the bed, I placed a set on each ankle and each wrist. Torri's brass bed featured both a wrap headboard and footboard that embraced the corners of the mattress, and with the care given to only the finest things, I assisted her with getting in the bed and requested she spread-eagle across the sheets. I took the open end of each of the handcuffs and closed them around the posts at each corner of the bed. Standing at the foot of the bed, I fixated my eyes on

Torri's svelte body as it appeared slightly suspended in air.

"You feeling OK, baby?" I asked. Her limbs seemed uncomfortably extended toward each post.

"I'm feeling fine," she said without hesitation.

The very peak of her pussy glistened from the wetness that had begun to trickle from her body. I climbed into the bed, onto my knees, and leaned into her groin, taking in her sensuous fragrance. Extending my tongue like a thirsty lizard, I traced the path in which her juices had flowed, from the bottom of her ankles to her navel. Tasting her, I massaged her skin with my lips until I got to the tips of her nipples, and it was there when I realized I could have Torri all night long and never want an ounce of sleep.

With my eyes open as I stroked Torri's breasts, I watched her lick her lips and listened to her suck her teeth. I moved toward her tantalizing protrusions and circled the outside of them with my tongue. I closed my circle with soft kisses to her face and then back to her lips again. For me, a kiss so early in the game was unheard of, but I couldn't resist.

Torri was my little secret, and I was willing to do whatever necessary to protect it. The time she and I spent together was a bit expensive, but she was worth it. Paulette, Chief of the ER at The Washington Hospital Center, worked all the time, and we never had the opportunity to go all out and just have fun with each other. One afternoon, I almost got caught when Torri showed up at my office in a black trench coat and stilettos.

"Senator, there is a Ms. Banks here to see you," Ryan, one of my interns, informed me with a huge grin on his face.

The smile on my face was even bigger than his as I hid behind the pages of *The Washington Post*. I hadn't seen her in about three weeks. I was up for re-election and was spending most of my time campaigning on the road and in the streets.

I calmly replied, "Tell her to take a seat, and I'll be with her in a few minutes."

My cell phone began vibrating against the top of the desk. I picked up the phone and saw it was Paulette.

"Will do," Ryan said, closing my door behind him. Ryan was at work every day and never missed a beat, but he was nosy as hell and stayed up in my business too much. All he ever did was sit in the lunchroom with the other interns and gossip about my calendar and my salacious, impromptu visitors. My other intern came in only twice a week and kept pretty much to herself.

Typically, Paulette doesn't call me at work, so her call was a bit of a surprise for me. "Hey, you," I answered with a bit of curiosity behind it. "What's up?"

"You," she said softly. "What are you doing?"

Sometimes I wondered if she'd planted a camera somewhere in my office because she always seemed to know when I was up to something. "Well, I'm sitting here reading *The Post* and about to see a constituent."

"Sounds boring. Guess where I am?"

"Uh, I don't know, honey. Tell me where you are."

"I'm coming down Constitution Avenue headed to your office."

FUCK! "You're on your way here?"

"Yeah, I thought I'd come and scoop you up, and we could head to Eastern Market for a bite to eat, and then maybe if you didn't have a lot on your schedule this afternoon, we could go home and get a quickie in."

Since I'd started fucking Torri, I didn't have much of a

need for a quickie, but I did have an idea. "Tell you what, you remember that time you asked me if I were inclined to do a threesome, and I told you hell no?"

She paused for a second. "Yes, I do remember that. Why? Have you changed your mind?"

"I've given it some thought, and well, I'm down with it, but I have to choose the girl."

Paulette's smile radiated through the phone. "I don't have a problem with that. Give me a time and place, and I'm there."

"OK. Three o'clock at the Marriot on Twenty-second and N."

"See you there."

Ryan left for a late lunch about thirty minutes after Torri had arrived, so I knew we were alone. I went out to the waiting area and saw her engaged in an issue of *Time* magazine. I was impressed to see she was doing more than flipping through the pictures. "What you reading, Ms. Girl?" I asked jokingly.

"Oh, I'm reading an article about the war. That's all."

"Bring your magazine on in here with you."

"OK." Tossing the magazine into the seat of her chair, Torri got up and followed me to my office. "I hope you're not angry with me for just showing up like this."

"Never," I replied gesturing for her to take a seat on the loveseat. "It's a pleasant surprise. You want me to take your coat?"

"You sure you want to do that?"

"I want you to be comfortable, and . . ."

Torri began untying the belt of her coat. In a matter of seconds, it hit the floor and all that was left was a red bra, a red G-string, a red garter, red thigh-highs, and red stilettos. Shit.

Strutting toward me, offering up every inch of her sexiness as she moved, Torri said to me, "I want you to be comfortable. You work too hard and need some excitement." She pushed me toward a barstool I used at the pub table near the window and began kissing my neck. "I've missed you, Senator."

Having Torri in my office had violated every oath I'd taken and every ethic I'd tried to protect or enforce. God knows I'd missed her over the last several weeks and wanted nothing more than this opportunity to make up for it. "Torri, baby, we can't do this here."

She wouldn't stop. Before I knew it, I was sitting on top of the barstool with Torri straddling my lap. "Can't do what, Senator?" she whispered in my ear, her pelvis gyrating against my abdomen.

"This. I could get into some pretty deep shit if we get caught. Now you don't want that, do you?" I returned her affections but quickly regained control of the situation by detaching her from my waist. I put my game face on. "Please stop."

Torri obliged and stopped the kisses and the fondling. "What's wrong?"

Getting up from the stool, I said, "Nothing's wrong. Ryan will be back any minute, and he never knocks. The last thing I need is for him to run to the other interns and tell them he caught me with someone who looks like a prostitute."

"That's what I am, aren't I?"

The young woman who usually had me beat on self-esteem was dealing herself a pretty low blow. "Where's that coming from?"

"Senator, you know that's what I am. A high-class whore that you're using to get what you want."

I walked over to the spot where Torri had dropped her coat. Dusting lint from the sleeves, I picked it up and covered her with it. "I'm not using you, Torri. I promise you that everyone is going to win here, especially you. Take a seat." It was easy to see that Torri had grown impatient with the process, and I realized I owed her more of an explanation.

"How's that supposed to happen, huh? How?"

"Just go along with the game for a minute. OK?"

"Hell no."

I wasn't about to lose this. I needed Torri. "The best thing for you to do is to continue being you. There is nothing you can really do right now. I need Earl to trust you more than he does now. He needs to trust you more than any of the other women he has working for him, and I can tell he trusts you quite a bit already. I also need you to keep seeing Roderick. I mean, be seen out in public with him and fuck his brains out if you have to."

"And what is all of this supposed to accomplish?"

"How accessible are the personnel files?"

"I don't know. I think Brandy has access to them."

"Don't want to deal with her."

"Those files are likely in Dee's office. Senator, I'm not like that with Dee. As a matter of fact, I—"

"I know. I know. You can't stand her. That's a good thing. It means I don't have to worry about you flipping on me and running to her with our plans."

"Shit, I don't even know what the plan is. Can you at least share that with me?"

I got up and closed the door to the outer office in case Ryan came back. Taking a seat next to Torri, I decided to let her in. "The personnel files have their birth certificates in them. I need to compare the information I have with what Earl has. My copies came directly from the health department, so I know what I have hasn't been tampered with."

Flustered, Torri consented, "I will see what I can do. Dee has that office on lock, and if I get caught snooping, she'd have me killed. She's just that much of a cold-hearted bitch."

"It'll be fine. I promise. By the way, I got my people looking for Niya."

"Really?" she asked, smiling.

"Be patient, grasshopper. In due time." I glanced at the clock on my desk and noticed it was near two. "Hey, you want to make some money?" Soon as that rolled off my tongue, I knew it was an insult.

"Excuse me? See what I meant? That's all you see when you see me. A high-class—"

"Torri, I didn't ask you that to insult you. A friend of mine and I wanted a bit of recreation this afternoon, and I want to know if you'd care to join us. I'd pay you the same thing I'd pay if we were at Allure."

"For real? Tip included?"

"Sure. Why not?"

Two hours later, I was sitting in a chair in Room 724 at the Marriott, watching Paulette get her pussy eaten out. Torri had Paulette's legs spread from one side of the bed to the other and literally had her nose mashed against Paulette's clit. I could hear the gurgles of cum seeping into Torri's mouth, and I must confess that sound is my one weakness.

Watching Paulette's eyes roll into the back of her head, I knew the shit was feeling good to her, and I wanted to experience it from my end.

I undressed in the spot where I stood and pulled my silver bullet from my briefcase. I walked over to the foot of the bed and lifted Torri's bottom toward me. Entering her first with my tongue, then with my fingers, I delicately spread open her lips and slid that steel rod inside of her until I heard her grunt and moan. In between her moments of excitement, Paulette was able to see my face as I pierced Torri's jewel over and over again. I leaned far enough over her backside to reach Paulette's lips, completing a circle of lust and compassion.

Torri:

A Quarter to Play

Three months into Senator Mabry's plan, things at Allure changed. Dee got fired, and Kimona was put in charge. I saw that change coming because Dee had stepped way of out control with the shit she was pulling. I, however, was blown away when Earl told me he was thinking about making some more changes, and those changes included me.

One thing I think Earl had forgotten was that I wasn't in this business to retire from it. I fell up in the joint because I needed a place to stay, and if I had to give up a piece of pussy to do it, then that's what I had to do.

Hooking me up with the mayor was Earl's way of showing me he trusted me; plus, it saved me from some of the true freaks the other girls serviced from time to time. The mayor had standing appointments; the rest of my time was devoted to the senator. She started coming in on the regular, and I really had no complaints, until the day Kimona called me into her office.

"Torri, we're going to make some changes. You will no longer be seeing the mayor."

My world was rocking. "What?"

"He's requested something different, and he went straight to Earl with it."

I knew she was feeding me bullshit. "You're lying, Kimona."

She picked up the phone and handed it to me. "You want to call Earl and let him tell you?" Walking toward me to take a seat on the corner of her desk, Kimona hung the phone back on its base. "These things happen. Men get bored, and we, as women, have to find ways to help them relieve that boredom. We must find ways to keep it fun and exciting for them." She chuckled.

I wasn't thinking too much about what I wanted for myself at that moment because I wanted Kimona's ass six feet under and didn't have a problem being the one who put her there. "You know what? I don't believe your cocky ass. I know you're up to something, and you better hope like a muthafucka I don't find out what it is."

As I prepared to leave, Kimona kept her eyes on me and watched every move I made. "Torri, you know, you and I can still kick it whenever you want. Based on your receipts, I see you been rockin' the senator's world."

"Whatever. By the way, who's the mayor going to be seeing now?"

Kimona strutted her ass back over to her chair and plopped down as if she wanted me to remember who the HBIC was. "Me," she replied conceitedly.

I'd promised Roderick I'd never call him, even though he had given me his cell number a while back. For as long as he had been seeing me, he promised he wanted to see no one but me, so this shit Kimona was dishing had some other motivation behind it. Why would he even risk it?

Cloaked by the impending darkness of dusk, I started out on my journey to City Hall. With every quarter I put into the machine to get my metro fare card, I heard the empty echoes of my life calling me. I got on the subway and watched those around me meandering through the simplest of lives. There was the white middle-aged businessman in his Brooks Brothers suit; the white woman dressed in a simple pair of slacks and a blouse, holding a book called *The Simple Plan*; the young brother bopping his head to the tunes of his iPod; and just toward the back was the young, black college girl—with books and backpack in tow, trying to figure out what it was the world was holding for her. Then, of course, there was me—a high-class whore with nothing to show for it.

I stared at my reflection in the window as we passed through the tunnels while the fading sunlight flickered in and out. At this point in my life, I, unlike everyone else in this shit, had nothing to lose.

I walked through security without a problem and headed toward the eighth floor, where the head of the mayor's security kept an office. Marcel and I were pretty cool, and he'd always told me to let him know if I needed anything—and he meant anything.

When I entered the office, Marcel was standing at the receptionist's desk laughing and talking with someone who looked old enough to be my grandmother. She peeked around Marcel's six-foot-eight frame and asked, "May I help you, dear?"

Marcel then turned around and flashed his huge grin

at me and gave me a wink, assuring me he was about to take care of me. "It's OK, June. I got it."

He ushered me into his office and closed the door behind us. It was in there that I let out a stream of tears, but was also able to exhale for a moment.

"What are you doing down here, Torri? You know—"

"I know, I know, I know. I needed to get out of there."

"So you came *here*?"

"I didn't have anybody else I thought I could trust. Is he bored with me?"

"What?"

"You heard me. Is he?"

"Where would you get some shit like that?"

"Kimona told me he was bored with me and wanted something different. She said he wanted to be with her."

"Ewww. That's nasty. She's nasty, and he can't stand her."

"I don't get it, Marcel. Something's going on. Why would she do that?"

"Baby girl, I have no idea. You want to talk to him?"

Oh, there was no way in hell I wanted Roderick to see me up here. He'd have a fit. "No, there's no need. He'd kill me if he saw me in here."

Marcel winked at me again. "Give me a second." He went outside and told that June lady she could go on home for the evening. Then he came back and opened up a big piece of furniture that looked like a bookcase. Inside of it, there were about twenty monitors tracking the mayor's every move.

"What's all this?"

"This is how we maintain surveillance on the mayor when he's in the building. You should feel pretty damn special because no one else gets to see this area." After saying that, he turned off all the monitors and pulled out his cell phone. "Can you come down here for a minute?"

Five minutes later, there was a knock at the private entrance to Marcel's office and in walked Roderick. His face went white as a sheet when he saw me. "What's going on? What are you doing down here?"

"Rod, man, hold up a sec. I think you need to hear her out before you start trippin'."

The mayor trusted any and everything Marcel brought to him. "OK."

Marcel asked, "Did Earl talk to you about switching up girls and seeing Kimona from now on?"

"What? Hell, no! You know I don't get down with that Kimona girl. She's bad news. Who told you that?"

I had no choice but to answer. "She told me that this afternoon and said you requested it."

Roderick came over to me, pulled the hood from my head, and kissed my forehead. "Baby, you mean too much to me for me to just toss you to the side like that." Then he took two steps back. "How are you and Rita getting along?"

"Uh, uh, uh. It's cool, I guess." I wasn't used to talking with others about the business of Allure, but it soon made sense to me that Rita and Roderick were my only two clients. "Why do you ask?"

"Oh, I was just wondering. I like the both of you and want to make sure you're both happy. So . . ."

"So . . . what?"

"I guess she's told you about what's going on."

"Yes, she did, and I told her I would do what I could. Does either one of you care if this plan backfires?"

"Yeah, I'm sure we both do, but with your help in all the right places, that will not happen. I'm still trying to get over this thing with Kimona."

"I'm telling you she's up to something, Rod," Marcel interjected.

Roderick had a way of raising his eyebrow when he was pondering something or when he was expecting an answer from you. "Tell you what . . . let Kimona switch with you. You know how I roll when I come to Allure, so you know nothing will happen to me. Right, Marcel?"

"Right."

Earl:

What the Fuck?

The mayor's call came at around midnight. These latenight calls would be the death of my marriage, but it was those calls that kept the lights on, helped Tina shop in the Gucci store, and paid the note on my S500.

"I need to see you."

"When and where?"

"Tomorrow morning in the National Air and Space Museum near the Star Trek exhibit at eleven o'clock. Don't be late."

As usual, he abruptly hung up.

When I arrived at the entrance of the museum, I saw members of the mayor's security detail all over the place. Inconspicuous to the average tourist, I noticed them whisper into their headsets as I walked past. At the start of the exhibit was a sign stating that it was closed for repairs. I instantly knew it was a set up because I'd just been there two days before with my son. Just inside the doorway, I saw silhouettes with glistening wrists. "Come on in, man. It won't take long," Marcel said.

As I was guided to the room where they show footage of the interviews with the cast members, the film started running.

Seconds later, the mayor appeared in the doorway. "I loved this show when I was growing up," he said, pointing to the screen.

"Yeah, um. Me too, man. What's up?"

Taking a seat next to me, the mayor pushed up on me to the point where I was beginning to feel uncomfortable. "I hear you got some catfighting going on over at Allure."

"What you mean, dawg?" I knew that no one but Dee had run her mouth. She's the only one with reason to.

"What happened to Dee?"

"Uh, she left. Moved on to bigger and better things."

"Hmph, that's strange. I thought Allure was the biggest and best there was."

"Yeah, heehee, it is." I stared at the floor. I glanced at the mayor out of the corner of my eye and saw that he wasn't laughing. "Man, you know how women get when they get their periods. They be out for one another's blood. It's like that in my own house with my wife and my daughter. Give them a piece of chocolate, and it's all good.

"OK. I see you want to be the comedian," the mayor commented. "What's up with your girl, Kimona, since it isn't a secret that's your bitch and all?"

"What you mean? She's holding it down, and I don't have any problems with her."

"So you trust her like that?"

"Well, yes, I do. She's got my best interest at heart."

I looked around the room and saw Marcel give the mayor the signal that they were almost out of time.

Suddenly the mayor grabbed me by wrist and began squeezing it as if he were trying to break it. "I'm going to take you at your word, and I want you to take me at mine. If she tries to screw with me anymore than what I've paid for, I'm going to kill her on the spot. Feel me?"

My bones felt like they were snapping. "OK, OK," I insisted. "Yo, man, what's up?"

"Everybody knows your girl is dirty, and if any of it gets on me, she's dead and so are you."

What the fuck?

After my meeting, I paced the Mall for a while, trying to sort out why Kimona was trying to move in on Torri's territory. I had given Kimona all of my attention and trust, but it seemed as if it wasn't enough for her. I found a bench and hit her up on her cell. "Whaddup, love? How are you?"

"I'm good, babe," she answered. "What's poppin'?'"

"Aw, nothing much. I, uh, was wondering if you had a minute to talk this morning."

"About what?"

"This whole Torri thing. I need to understand what you got against her."

"Honestly, she's too new to have the kind of clout she has."

"Could it be that you're just jealous? I mean, you came to Allure —"

"Don't be bringing that up again. I know how I started, and I also know what I did to get mine. Torri walks her ass up in here, and you give her the mayor right off the bat. She ain't have shit to prove to you, and that wasn't right."

"You know, Kimona, I think you could learn a thing or two from Torri. She has never run to me complaining about all that madness you and Dee put her through. She has kept her mouth shut, and I would really appreciate that right now from you."

"What the hell is that supposed to mean?"

"What I mean is, all my business is out in the streets, and it shouldn't be going down like that. After all I do for you and the others, this is the thanks I get?"

"Earl, stop talking in riddles. What are you getting at?"

"Look, don't be switching up on the mayor. He's my biggest client, and I don't want to make him unhappy."

"Too late. I've already dismissed Torri for the evening. She won't even be in the building."

"Kimona, you had no right!"

"The hell you say. I have every right. I run this mutha, remember?"

What could I say? I had created this monster, and without erasing her from the face of the earth, I had no way of stopping her. "You better watch yourself, Kimona. You're playing a dangerous game, and I can't protect you when you don't play by the rules." Pissed to high hell with the woman that could've once been Mrs. Earl Dixon, I hung up the phone.

At that moment it hit me. I knew what Kimona was scheming. I'd managed to catch her trying to run this game on me a time or two. *Damn, her ass has gone too far this time.*

I called the OB-GYN's office and asked the date of Kimona's last period. Shaun, one of the office assistants, looked up Kimona's records. She had just had her period two weeks ago and should be ovulating right now. That was all I needed to hear. She was on her own.

Kimona:

An Eye on the Prize

Earl can be so gullible sometimes, and I attribute that to his weakness for pussy. Sure, it's OK to sleep with the help, but you got to know who you working with. He fell for that whole thing with Dee, and, as it turned out, I ended up on top. I got that bitch out of here. Now Allure is all but mine. Everybody thinks I've had my eye on running this place for the money and the prestige. Guess I've done OK up to this point. The girls around here give me more love than Dee ever got. We have a good time and treat our clients well. No one, including Earl, has reason to question me about anything.

Tina, Earl's wife, stopped by the office one morning and wanted to talk about plans for the business.

I'd changed my mind about Cherry and was willing to explain my decision to not have an assistant at all. "Are you two still set on this percentage crap?"

"Yes, we are. This is too much for just one person."

"Girl, I got this. You and Earl better recognize."

"Anyway, did you get someone else, or is it going to be Torri?"

"It's not going to be Torri. I don't want another Brandy running through here."

"I don't see her being like that. She's really a sweet girl, and besides, I know she's the only one of you skanks who hasn't slept with my husband."

"Well, I don't need her. I don't need anybody."

"When was the last time you talked to Earl?"

"Shit, a few days ago, I think. He wasn't looking too good. Is he sick?"

"Not that I know of. He's got a lot on his plate. He told me you're going to start seeing the mayor, instead of Torri."

"Yeah, he requested it and—"

"The mayor? Requested you? Give me a fucking break," Tina snorted, almost sounding indignant. "He's got way too much class for you."

"Whatever. Tell your boy he doesn't have to worry about Allure, because it's all gravy from here on out. I got this kitty on lock."

"I don't know, Kimona. Something just doesn't feel right."

Tina had always been a paranoid woman who always thought someone was going to steal her man and their bank account. To tell you the truth, if I hadn't come up with this master plan, then I might have taken Earl and their money too. She'd spent over three hours in my office trying to convince me to make Torri my assistant, but I wasn't having it.

I eventually had to put her ass out so I could get ready for my appointment with the mayor. His security detail came through about seven-thirty to check out my apartment. We'd done away with all the video cameras and junk like that because it was simply bad business.

The mayor arrived exactly at eight o'clock, choosing not to make his usual stop at the bar.

I met him in the hallway outside my apartment. "Good evening," I offered.

"Hello," he said, passing by in a huff.

Following him to the room, I watched him stop by the door. "Had a bad day?"

"No, I'm fine. Been looking forward to relaxing."

I opened the door, and he let me enter first.

"Well, I'm going to make sure you do just that."

He closed the door and dropped his clothes right in the middle of my floor.

"In a hurry?"

"No, I always get naked the minute I walk inside. That's how I begin to relax."

I could literally see the blood rushing to the tip of his dick. It jostled up and down like a water balloon. "You want something to drink?"

"Oh, no. I don't drink. You should've gotten that from Torri. Come to think of it, though, I'll have a little something non-alcoholic."

I turned to the bar and made him a glass of cranberry juice and ginger ale. I slipped a pill of E in it. "Well, Torri's not available tonight, so she asked me to step in for her. I suggest you do something different, so you can see all the variety that Allure has to offer."

"Actually, I *would* like to do something a bit different tonight."

"Anything you want, Mr. Mayor."

"I like to reward my employees every now and again

for their loyalty, so tonight I'm going to do just that by having one of them join me."

I wasn't expecting that to come out of his mouth, but I'd told him he could have anything he wanted. "Not a problem."

The mayor picked up his phone, and, within seconds, there was a knock at my door.

I opened it to find a six-foot eight giant on the other side. "Come on in. The more the merrier."

Without exception, condoms are required at Allure whenever penetration occurs. Big Boy came in, immediately whipped out his dick, and wrapped a condom around it. He grabbed me and plunged my ass right down on it. Working me up and down, my muscles hadn't had a chance to get ready for him. He, by far, had one of the widest penises I'd ever had in me. I knew he had ripped something along the way, but I took it like the champ I knew I was.

When he got ready to pop off, he looked me square in the eye and grabbed the back of my neck with one hand and the top of my waist with the other. Pressing me against him, he released and lifted me from him.

"Had enough?" the mayor asked. "I still get my turn, don't I?" While his "employee" was in the bathroom flushing, my star client sat there with his condom-covered rod at full attention.

Staggering and still trying to get my bearings, I replied, "Of course, you do. That's what you paid for."

"Turn around and bend over."

I backed up to him and perched myself atop his groin and let him bone me like a Rottweiler in heat.

He reached from behind me to squeeze my titties until

he nutted. I held my legs together tightly so that when I moved the condom came with me.

By now, the mayor was too out of it to realize what I had done. Big Boy was still in the bathroom when I called out to him to come and help get the Mayor dressed.

"I hate to rush him out like this, but I have another appointment in thirty minutes."

Big Boy tried to help the mayor up and couldn't understand why he was so out of it. "Did you give him something?"

"No, I didn't. He busted a nut and fell right out. That's what happens when you get good pussy around here. You done in the bathroom?"

"Yeah."

"OK, well, I need to use it. You two can show yourselves out, can't you?"

"No problem."

The cum was oozing down my thighs. I grabbed a piece of cardboard from my tampon box, scraped it into a cup, and pulled the condom from my pussy. I emptied its contents into the cup and covered it with a top. Just then, there was knock at the door, with someone trying to turn the knob.

"Hold on, hold on," I persisted, but the person on the other side was impatient.

I flushed the condom down the toilet and threw the cup in the medicine cabinet. "Damn, what is it?" I snapped, yanking the door open.

"The condom," Big Boy asked. "I need that condom."

For the first time in my life, I was scared. "I don't have it. I just flushed it down the toilet."

With his trained eyes, he spotted the tiny drips of

semen on the black granite sink and on the black porcelain toilet.

For a minute, I thought I was going to get away with my plan to have the mayor's bastard child. But Big Boy pushed me aside and started going through the cabinets below the counter, and then through the medicine cabinet. It didn't help matters much that the damn syringe was right next to the cup.

Shaking his head, Big Boy said disgustedly, "Now, Miss Kimona, I see you've been a naughty girl."

I didn't get up that morning with the thought of being dead by the end of the day on my mind. Come to think of it, who does?

The Mayor:

HNIC

Typically, I try not to say much until I'm fucked with. Folks try to trip you up on words, and shit you put on paper. That's why I keep my mouth shut, and I have at least five people look over my shit before it's sent out. Then you got muthafuckas who want to try to take you down because they're hating on you for what you got, and let's not forget the Kimonas of the world who try to trap a man by stealing his juice when she thinks he isn't looking.

Earl is no fool. The second he got off the phone with the gynecologist he called me to give me a heads-up. Alerting Kimona to the fact that he knew what she was up to would make matters worse and cause unnecessary drama and tension. There was no telling which way her tongue was going to roll if she was crossed and started talking, so it was best to shut her up before she got the chance.

Marcel got Earl on the phone for me. I don't know how he did it, but he drove from River Road in Potomac,

Maryland to downtown DC in less than twenty minutes. When he saw Kimona's lifeless body resting against a stack of pillows, he hung his head for a second and then walked over to her and closed her eyelids.

Turning to me, he asked calmly, "Was there any way around this?"

Coldly, I replied, "No, Marcel caught her in the bathroom with the sperm and the syringe. It was best for everybody, especially you. You know she could have destroyed you too, Earl." Marcel, in one swift move before she could open her mouth to scream, had snapped Kimona's neck.

"Man, but did y'all have to kill her?"

I felt this nigga getting a little soft on me. "Earl, please don't tell me you had feelings for this whore. They're all whores."

He looked up at me after leaning over to kiss Kimona on the forehead and asked, "Even Torri? You know Torri works here too. You remember that, don't you?"

"Torri's not the issue here, and I can't believe you're starting to whine like an old bitch."

"So what's to be done with her? You know we can't call anyone."

Did this boy not know who I was? Had he forgotten who helped him get Allure's doors open? "Well, I did. Rita and Paulette will be here shortly."

"Who's Paulette?"

"Rita's wife. She's a doctor and can help us dispose of this mess as neatly as possible."

"Aw, man. Awww, man."

"Why don't you get yourself something to drink?"

Earl walked over to the bar and made himself two shot glasses full of Patrón.

I covered up Kimona's body with a sheet that Marcel

had gotten from the closet. "It's a shame she was so dumb."

"What you mean?"

"She was actually thinking she'd drugged me by putting some E in my cranberry juice. I saw her when she did it. If she'd really done her homework, she would've known I don't drink anything when I get up to the apartment."

"Man, what are we going to do with her? She can't stay here like this."

I sat on the chair as Marcel began cleaning the bathroom and disposing of all traces of my DNA. "Earl, dude, calm the hell down. I keep trying to tell you there's nothing to worry about. You keep forgetting who's the head nigga in charge."

The Senator:

A Necessary Evil

Paulette and I rode up I-95 in complete silence. Before leaving the house, I told her what was going on, and, needless to say, she was reluctant for us to get our hands dirty. She knew Rod was my boy, and I'd do anything—and I mean anything—to help him out if I could. I took every precaution I could to make sure we weren't noticed. Instead of going into town and risk parking anywhere near Allure, I decided to park at the Franconia Station, leave the car, and take the Metro.

Paulette broke her silence the minute we pulled into the parking space and turned the car off. "This is a bad idea, Rita, and you know it."

Adjusting my hat in the rearview mirror, I said, "It is not. Rod's thorough, and so am I."

"Maybe, but what if something goes wrong?"

"If you cooperate, nothing will happen. Just go in there, clean the girl's pussy out, and make sure there isn't a trace of DNA on her."

"Rita, there's no way to do that and know for sure that you've gotten it all. Did they rape her or something?"

"No, they didn't, and you know better to even ask anything like that. She was trying to steal Rod's semen, and she got caught."

"Serves his ass right for cheating on that sexy-ass wife of his."

"Uh, she isn't a saint. Her ass has got some skeletons in her closet too."

"Whatever you say. I'm not going to do this. I can't risk it."

"Risk what? Your career? Please. You've got some nerve."

Paulette used to have her own OB-GYN practice and was almost sued. One of her patients reported to the authorities that Paulette had fondled her during a pelvic exam. Fortunately, the woman had a history of making false complaints against professionals, and no one at the medical licensing board or the district attorney's office would listen to her.

Soon after she met me, Paulette and I were playing truth or dare while under the influence of Hawaiian weed and tequila, and I asked her what really happened that day. I was shocked when Paulette admitted she'd been attracted to the woman and actually got in a feel or two during the exam. The only two people in the world who knew that were me and Paulette, and although I loved Paulette tremendously, I'd do what I had to do to protect Roderick.

"Now you know you have a skeleton or two in your closet, so you have no right to be acting like this. I'm sure you don't want to lose your license, do you?"

Paulette gasped. "Are you threatening me, Rita?"

"You know I don't make threats."

At that point, she absolutely had no choice but to do what I'd asked.

The train ride into the city was just as tense and silent as the ride to the station. We got off at the Foggy Bottom stop and walked to Allure with Paulette's doctor bag in tow.

In all our years together, I'd never asked what was inside of it, but I was certain it contained whatever we needed to make this operation go down smoothly.

Marcel greeted us at the door of Kimona's apartment. He had the same stern look on his face as usual.

In the bedroom is where I found Earl, Rod, and Kimona's corpse.

"Anybody see you?" Earl asked.

"No."

"Good. I'm Earl," he said, extending his hand toward Paulette. Even in the toughest of situations, he was always professional and courteous.

"Likewise. I'm Paulette," she offered in return.

Rod, standing there in a dress shirt and jeans, walked over to her and opened his arms for their usual hug. "Don't let the environment change our friendship, girl. You know you make the best fried chicken in Virginia, and I'm still your biggest fan. Give me some love."

Reluctantly, Paulette gave him a hug and asked, "What are you about to get us into?"

"Not shit, if all goes well. I need you to make this happen."

"I'll see what I can do, but I'm going to need everyone out of the room."

Only Marcel stayed behind with her. The rest of us went into the living room and sat down. I didn't care one way or another about the bitch being dead because she was a troublemaker and deserved everything she got; I'm sure Rod felt the same. Earl, though, was a different case. He was sitting there like he'd lost his best friend, and I couldn't understand why he felt that way about someone who could destroy him.

"Earl, man, are you going to be OK?"

With his head buried in the palms of his hands, he replied, "I'm going to have to be. Are you sure she is going to—"

"Paulette has it under control. I'm sure of it. So what are you going to do about the business? Who are you going to have in charge?"

"Well, I was thinking about Torri. I trust her, and I know she wouldn't do anything stupid like this. She's just not that kind of girl."

"I agree, but I don't think this business is for her. She's a really smart young lady, and I know she wants more out of life than being somebody's whore. What do you think, Rod?"

The mayor, for his own selfish reasons, had a difference of opinion. "Torri is a good girl, and I really like her. Running this place is a lot for someone her age. You should ask her to help out a bit until you find a suitable replacement."

Earl looked to me for a rebuttal, but, shit, I was boning Torri too. I was absolutely crazy about her but was willing to let the sex go so she could have a life. Then, too, if she worked for Earl for a little while, she could get those files for me. *Is it really going to be that easy?*

"Earl, look, I don't know how much you've talked to her, but Torri wants a better life than what Allure could ever give to her. I was thinking, like Rod, that maybe you could let her run the place until you can get somebody else up in here. One thing I want to do, though, is get Torri in school somewhere."

"School?" Rod interrupted. "What the hell you mean?"

"Male chauvinistic asshole. If I have anything to do with it, she'll be in college at the beginning of the semester. Torri has the brains to run this place, and as you can see, Earl, it's those uneducated hoochies that have you in this mess in the first place. Let Torri run things part-time, and go to school when she's not here. Give her a break from the sex to allow her the opportunity to make something of herself."

Rod was pissed. "How the hell can you ask him to do something like that? I mean . . ."

Just as Rod was about to lose it, Earl came out of nowhere with the shock of the century. "What will this mean for your investigation, senator, if I agree to what you're suggesting?"

The look on my face said it all. "I'm not sure I know what you're talking about."

"Come on, senator, you should know better. I'm Earl Dixon. I'm surprised at you. You oughta know who you're fucking with before you even begin the game." He stood and walked over to the counter, where Kimona had several bottles of liquor stored. Picking up a bottle of Hennessy, he poured himself a glass and downed it straight.

"If there were an 'investigation,' how do you know anything about it? There are only two other people who would know what's going on, and one of them is sitting in this room."

Rod had put on his poker face, and I knew he wasn't going to utter a word. Torri had too much to lose with her desire to find Niya, so I knew she hadn't said anything. Earl had to be calling my bluff.

"I don't think you know shit, Earl."

"Oh, you don't? I've got three of your colleagues in this building right now. A couple of them are so far in debt with trying to maintain their All-American dream that they can't even cough up enough cash to get a blow job. Got kids in private school and college, behind on the mortgage, running from the repo man. Another cashed in part of his 401K, so he could have one night in this place. And that's where your boy Earl, comes in. I am the fulfiller of dreams—I make shit happen. Feel me?"

"What do you want?"

"Call off your dogs, and leave me alone."

"And if I don't?"

"I haven't decided yet. I need to know who your rat is. I want to think it was Kimona."

Well, all was not lost. He was still in the dark.

Minutes later, the bedroom door opened, and Paulette emerged with Marcel right behind her. "It's done. I'm finished."

"No disrespect, Paulette, but I'm going to have to check her."

"No need. Marcel already did, and she's clean. There isn't a trace of anything on her. How do you plan to dispose of the body?"

Finally, Rod spoke. "Already taken care of. Marcel will handle it. All he needs to know is where to ship her. I suggest we send her somewhere where no one will give a damn about her or how she got there."

Earl chuckled as he swirled the last swig of his third shot of Henny around in the bottom of its glass. "Send her home."

Torri: Payday

Kimona's disappearance wasn't a surprise to me. With all the players involved, I knew we'd never see or hear from her again. Earl asked me to step in for a while until he could sort out the management of Allure, and I didn't mind at all. It gave me a chance to see what it was like to be in charge. If you ask me, it was a bit overrated.

One thing I did have an opportunity to do was get the personnel files the senator wanted. I met her at the zoo to deliver them to her. She told me there were some things she wanted to talk over with me and didn't want to do it within the confines of Allure.

I found her sitting inside the reptile house reading an issue of *The City Paper*.

"Hey," I said standing there in my BabyPhat fleece warm-up suit with my Dolce and Gabbana sunglasses shielding my eyes.

"Hey, yourself, beautiful. How you doing?"

"I'm good. Can we go sit outside at the snack bar or something? I don't do snakes too well."

"Oh, sure," she said, getting up from the concrete.

We walked over to the snack area and found a seat in the back.

"How's it been going for you?"

"I don't like it. The business side of it is cool, you know, handling the money, the bills, and the clients. I've kinda outgrown the sex part of it." I handed her the files in a Louis Vuitton tote bag. "You can keep the bag as a gift." I smiled.

She and I had stopped seeing each other after it had gotten out that the mayor's wife had been frequenting a brothel in northwest DC. To protect his own ass, he stopped coming by as well. It didn't make any difference to me, though. I was tired of all of it.

"Thank you. I wanted to talk to you about something since we're here."

"OK."

"What would you think about going to college in the District? There are plenty to choose from, and I could help make it happen for you."

"College? Are you serious?"

"Yes, I am. The mayor and I talked about it last night, and he's willing to do whatever he can to help."

"What about Earl?"

"He's cool with it too. You can run Allure and go to school part-time if you want."

College. I'd always imagined it but thought I'd never be able to go. "So who's going to pay for it? I have money, but—"

"Don't worry about that. We've got you covered."

In many ways, I didn't trust the senator because I had yet to see Niya, and I refused to ask about her. I shouldn't have to remind her of her promises. I do, however, remember telling her I didn't always want to be somebody's whore. It's interesting to see she remembered that. "Wow. I would love to go."

"Once you've selected where you want to go, we've got to get your paperwork completed. You'll be able to start next semester."

"What's going to happen with this investigation regarding Earl? I think you should—"

"That is no longer your problem."

Relieved, I smiled and reached out to hug her. We embraced and held one another for several seconds. My eyes watered because, for once, I'd found someone who believed in me and wanted to genuinely see me become something more than a politician's whore. In time, I could forgive her for not letting Niya materialize. It must've never been meant to be.

"Thank you, thank you so much."

"You're more than welcome. Hey, by the way, did you ever get to meet my other intern?"

"No, I didn't. I only met that guy."

"That's right, you did. Well, she came out here with me today to get out of the office for a minute. If you don't mind, I would like you to say hello to her."

I'd bent over to tie my shoe. When I lifted my head, I could do nothing but scream. "Oh, my God! Oh, my God! Oh. My. GOD!"

"Torri, meet my assistant, Niya."

The Cat House. It had its advantages after all.

About the Authors

Anna J.

Anna J is an erotica writer from Philly who also walks the runway in her spare time as a full-figured model. Co-author of *Stories to Excite You: Menage Quad,* Anna put her writing skills to the test in this hot collaboration that was released during the fall of 2004.

Her debut novel, *My Woman His Wife*, is high on the charts and a good read for those who enjoy a steamy love affair with a little bit of drama to boot. And if your Anna J. cravings still aren't satisfied you can also find another hot story of hers in *Fetish*: *A Compilation of Erotic Stories, The Aftermath*, and *Get-Money Chicks*, all available in bookstores nationwide. Anna J. was born and raised in Philly, where she still resides, and is working on her next novel, the forthcoming *My Little Secret*.

Brittani Williams

Brittani Williams was born and raised in Philadelphia, PA, where she currently resides. She began writing when a school assignment required her to write a short play. This assignment showed her how far her imagination could go.

She started out writing short stories in play script form until deciding to take a plunge at changing the format to that of a novel. After doing some research and finding out how hard it was to get a publishing deal, she briefly gave up on writing. After attending college and switching majors a few times, she decided to get back to writing when she got an idea for an exciting story.

Next she self-published a short story to get feedback, and when the response was good, she decided to write a novel-length version of it. After more research she came across Q-Boro Books' website and submitted her manuscript. They quickly responded and soon gave her a book deal.

Brittani thanks Mark Anthony and the entire Q-Boro staff for giving her the opportunity to show the world what her family and friends have raved about since day one.

She is currently majoring in Education and Fashion Design in Philadelphia. Brittani is the mother of a three-year-old and is also hard at work on her third novel, *Black Diamond,* to be released in December 2008. Stay tuned!

Laurinda D. Brown

When you do what your passion is—your passion being what God gave you the zest and talent to do—the rest falls into place.

Divine destiny is what motivates mother, daughter, author Laurinda D. Brown to do what she does—write novels that portray real people in real-life situations. "Growing up in

Memphis, TN, and graduating from Howard University exposed me to the diverse sides of human nature and gave me the opportunity to observe people and their situations. I wrote to work through my own emotions, to find explanations for other people's circumstances, and to try to humanize thier idiosyncrasies. Writing expresses my take on the world."

Laurinda's books include *Fire & Brimstone,* the 2005 Lamda Literary Award finalist for Best Debut Lesbian Fiction, and *Undercover.*

The author currently resides with her two daughters in Hampton Roads, Virginia, where she continues to write about life—not lifestyles. She firmly believes that one day we will love one another not for what we are, but for who we are.

Check out Laurinda online at: www.ldbrownbooks.com

SNEAK PREVIEW OF

My Little Secret

by Anna J.

Coming in September 2008

Ask Yourself

Ask yourself a question . . . Have you ever had a session of love making? Do you want me? Have you ever been to heaven?
~Raheem DeVaughn

February 9th, 2007

She feels like melted chocolate on my fingertips. The same color from the top of her head to the very tips of her feet. Her nipples are two shades darker than the rest of her, and they make her skin the perfect backdrop against her round breasts. Firm and sweet like two ripe peaches dipped in baker's chocolate, they are a little more than a handful and greatly appreciated. Touching her makes me feel like I've finally found peace on earth, and there is no feeling in the world greater than that.

Right now her eyes are closed and her bottom lip is tightly tucked between her teeth. From my viewpoint, between her widely spread legs I can see the beginnings of yet another orgasm playing across her angelic face. These are the moments that make it all worthwhile. Her perfectly arched eyebrows go into a deep frown, and her eyelids flutter slightly. When her head falls back I know she's about to explode.

I move up on my knees so that we are pelvis to pelvis. Both of us are dripping wet from the humidity and the situation. Her legs are up on my shoulders, and her hands are cupping my breasts. I can't tell where her skin begins or where mine ends. As I look down at her, and watch her face go through way too many emotions I smile a little bit. She always did love the dick, and since we've been together she's never had to go without it. Especially since the one I have never goes down.

I'm pushing her tool into her soft folds inch by inch as if it were really a part of me, and her body is alive. I say "her tool" because it belongs to her, and I just enjoy using it on her. Her hip-length dreads seem to wrap us in a cocoon of coconut oil and sweat, body heat and moisture, soft moans and tear drops, pleasure and pain, until we seemingly burst into an inferno of ecstasy.

Our chocolate skin is searing to the touch and we melt into each other, becoming one. I can't tell where hers begins . . . I can't tell where mine ends.

She smiles . . . her eyes are still closed and she's still shaking from the intensity. I take this opportunity to taste her lips, and to lick the salty sweetness from the side of her neck. My hands begin to explore, and my tongue encircles her dark nipples. She arches her back when my full lips close around her nipple, and I begin to suck softly as if she's feeding me life from within her soul.

Her hands find their way to my head and become tangled in my soft locks, identical to hers but not as long. I push into her deep, and grind softly against her clit in search of her "J-spot" because it belongs to me, Jada. She speaks my name so soft that I barely hear her. I know she wants me to take what she so willingly gave me, and I want to hear her beg for it.

I start to pull back slowly, and I can feel her body tightening up, trying to keep me from moving. One of many soft moans is heard over the low hum of the clock radio that sits next to our bed. I hear slight snatches of Raheem DeVaughn singing about being in heaven, and I'm almost certain he wrote that song for me and my lady.

I open her lips up so that I can have full view of her sensitive pearl. Her body quakes with anticipation from the feel of my warm breath touching it, my mouth just mere inches away. I blow cool air on her stiff clit, causing her to tense up briefly, her hands taking hold of my head, trying to pull me closer. At this point my mouth is so close to her, all I would have to do is twitch my lips to make contact, but I don't. I want her to beg for it.

My index finger is making small circles against my own clit, my honey sticky between my legs. The ultimate pleasure is giving pleasure, and I've experienced that on both accounts. My baby can't wait anymore, and her soft pants are turning into low moans. I stick my tongue out, and her clit gladly kisses me back.

Her body responds by releasing a syrupy sweet slickness that I lap up until it's all gone, fucking her with my tongue the way she likes it. I hold her legs up and out to intensify her orgasm because I know she can't handle it that way.

"Does your husband do you like this?" I ask between licks. Before she could answer I wrap my full lips around her clit and suck her into my mouth, swirling my tongue around her hardened bud, causing her body to shake.

Snatching a second toy from the side of the bed, I take one hand to part her lips, and I ease her favorite toy (The Rabbit) inside of her. Wishing that the strap-on I was wearing was a real dick so that I could feel her pulsate, I turn the toy on low at first, wanting her to receive the ultimate pleasure. In the dark room the glow-in-the-dark toy is lit brightly, the light disappearing inside of her when I push it all the way in.

The head of the curved toy turns in a slow circle while the pearl beads jump around on the inside, hitting up against her smooth walls during insertion. When I push the toy in, she pushes her pelvis up to receive it, my mouth latched on to her clit like a vise. She moans louder, and I kick the toy up a notch to medium, much to her delight.

Removing my mouth from her clit, I rotate between flicking my wet tongue across it to heat it, and blowing my breath on it to cool it, bringing her to yet another screaming orgasm, followed by strings of *"I love you"* and *"Please don't stop."*

Torturing her body slowly, I continue to stimulate her clit, pushing her toy in and out of her on a constant rhythm. When she lifts her legs to her chest I take the opportunity to let the ears on the rabbit toy that we are using do its job on her clit, while my tongue find its way to her chocolate ass. I bite one cheek at a time replacing it with wet kisses, sliding my tongue in between to taste her there. Her body squirming underneath me lets me know I've hit the jackpot, and I fuck her with my tongue there also.

She's moaning, telling me in a loud whisper that she can't take it anymore. That's my cue to turn the toy up high. The buzzing from the toy matches that of the radio, and with her moans and my pants mixed in, we sound like a well-rehearsed orchestra singing a symphony of passion. I allow her to buck against my face while I keep up with the rhythm of the toy, her juice oozing out the sides and forming a puddle under her ass. I'm loving it.

She moans and shakes until the feeling in the pit of her stomach subsides and she is able to breathe at a normal rate. My lips taste salty-sweet from kissing her body while she tries to get her head together, rubbing the sides of my body up and down in a lazy motion.

Valentine's Day is fast approaching, and I have a wonderful evening planned for the two of us. She already promised me that her husband wouldn't be an issue because he'll be out of town that weekend, and besides all that, they haven't celebrated Cupid's day since the year after they were married. So I didn't even think twice about it. After seven years it should be over for them anyway.

"It's your turn now," she says to me in a husky lust-filled voice, and I can't wait for her to take control.

The ultimate pleasure is giving pleasure, and, man, does it feel good both ways.

She starts by rubbing her oil-slicked hands over the front of my body, taking extra time around my sensitive nipples before bringing her hands down across my flat stomach.

I've since then removed the strap-on dildo, and am completely naked under her hands. I can still feel her sweat on my skin, and I can still taste her on my lips. Closing my eyes I enjoy the sensual massage that I'm being treated to. After two years of us making love it's still good and gets better every time.

She likes to take her time covering every inch of my

body, and I enjoy letting her. She skips past my love box, and starts at my feet, massaging my legs from the toes up. When she gets to my pleasure point, her fingertips graze the smooth, hairless skin, quickly teasing me, before she heads back down, and does the same thing with my other limb. My legs are spread apart and lying flat on the bed with her in between, relaxing my body with ease. A cool breeze from the cracked window blows across the room every so often, caressing my erect nipples, making them harder than before, until her hands warm them back up again.

She knows when I can't take anymore, and she rubs and caresses me until I am begging her to kiss my lips. I can see her smile through half-closed eyelids, and she does what I requested. Dipping her head down between my legs she kisses my lips just as I asked, using her tongue to part them so that she could taste my clit.

My body goes into mini-convulsions on contact and I am fighting a battle to not cum that I never win.

"Valentine's Day belongs to us, right?" I ask her again between moans. I need her to be here. V-Day is for lovers, and she and her husband haven't been that in ages. I deserve it . . . I deserve her. I just don't want this to be a repeat of Christmas or New Year's Eve.

"Yes, it's yours," she says, between kisses on my thigh and sticking her tongue inside of me. Two of her fingers find their way inside of my tight walls, and my pelvic area automatically bounces up and down on her hand as my orgasm approaches.

"Tell me you love me," I say to her as my breathing becomes raspy. Fire is spreading across my legs and working its way up to the pit of my stomach. I need her to tell me before I explode.

"I love you," she says, and at the moment she places

her tongue in my slit, I release my honey all over her tongue.

It feels like I am on the Tea Cup ride at the amusement park as my orgasm jerks my body uncontrollably. It feels like the room is spinning. She is sucking and slurping my clit while the weight of her body holds the bottom half of me captive. I'm practically screaming and begging her to stop, and just when I think I'm about to check out of here, she lets my clit go.

I take a few more minutes to get my head together, allowing her to pull me into her and rub my back. It's moment s like this that makes it all worthwhile.

We lay like that for a while longer, listening to each other breathe, and much to my dismay she slides my head from where it was resting on her arm and gets up out of the bed.

I don't say a word. I just lie on the bed and watch her get dressed. I swear, everything she does is so graceful, like there's a rhythm riding behind it.

Pretty soon she is dressed and standing beside the bed, looking down at me.

She smiles and I smile back, not worried, because she promised me our lover's day, and that's only a week away.

"So, Valentine's Day belongs to me, right?" I ask her again, just to be certain.

"Yes, it belongs to you."

We kiss one last time, and I can still taste my honey on her lips. She already knows the routine, locking the bottom lock behind her. Just thinking about her makes me so horny, and I pick up her favorite toy to finish the job. Five more days, and it'll be on again.